Clement Ferdinand Heverly

History of Monroe Township and Borough, 1779-1885

With biographical sketches of the pioneers: her soldiers, and statistics, and matters

of general interest connected with the township

Clement Ferdinand Heverly

History of Monroe Township and Borough, 1779-1885
*With biographical sketches of the pioneers: her soldiers, and statistics, and matters of
general interest connected with the township*

ISBN/EAN: 9783337308537

Printed in Europe, USA, Canada, Australia, Japan

Cover: Foto ©Raphael Reischuk / pixelio.de

More available books at **www.hansebooks.com**

HISTORY

OF

◄ MONROE ►

TOWNSHIP AND BOROUGH.

1779--1885

WITH

BIOGRAPHICAL SKETCHES OF THE PIONEERS.

HER SOLDIERS

AND

STATISTICS AND MATTERS OF GENERAL INTEREST
CONNECTED WITH THE TOWNSHIP.

BY

C. F. HEVERLY.

—§—

TOWANDA, PA.:

REPORTER-JOURNAL PRINTING COMPANY.

1885.

PREFACE.

This volume has been written as a souvenir to posterity—that the deeds and virtues of the heroic pioneers may ever be kept bright—and that we may learn to cherish the names of "the Fathers and Mothers," more and more, as they grow old, for the many valuable lessons their lives have taught us, and for the hardships and privations, which they so nobly bore that we might enjoy the fruits and blessings of their labors. Accordingly this volume is most affectionately dedicated to the pioneers, our benefactors, the men and women who founded the settlements, made the country what it is, and the men and boys who offered their lives to save our country from disunion. In conclusion, the author tenders his greatest obligations to the following, who have most generously assisted in furnishing data :

A. L. Cranmer, Esq., J. R. Irvine, Nathan Northrup, Wm. Northrup, John Northrup, Henry Northrup, W. A. Kellogg, Lovina Kellogg, P. E. Alden, J. W. Irvine, Mrs. Geo. Tracy, Mrs. T. T. Smiley, Mrs. E. F. Young, Samuel Lyon, Lyman Marcy, Samuel Cole, Mrs. J. L. Rockwell, Freeman Sweet, J. H. Lewis, J. F. Woodruff, Mrs. J. F. Woodruff, Emily Robbins, J. H. Summers, S. S. Merithew, Mrs. David

Ridgeway, Wm. Irvine, W. W. Fowler, Benjamin North, G. L. Bull, Dr. O. H. Rockwell, H. W. Rockwell, Jos. Bull, Chas. Hollon, Mrs. Chas. Brown, J. W. Lewis, Martin Cranmer, Joab Summers, Mrs. Joab Summers, T. T. Smiley, E. W. Stevens, O. M. Brock, H. H. Ingham, E. E. Mingos, Monroe; Mrs. Robert Bull, Robert Bull, Asylum; O. N. Salisbury, Beech Creek, Pa.; Capt. G. V. Myer, Dr. D. N. Newton, Capt. J. A. Wilt, Mrs. Wm. B. Dodge, D. J. Sweet, Benj. Northrup, Mrs. G. H. Watkins, Prothonotary W. J. Young, John J. Spalding, John G. Culver, clerks, Towanda; Rev. David Craft, Wyalusing, Pa.; Mrs. Dr. J. E. Ingham, Corning, N. Y.; Mrs. Jos. Lippincott, Joliet, Ill.; Miss Jane D. Irvine, Warren, Pa.; Mrs. Nelson Parker, Bradford, Pa.; B. S. Dartt, Canton, Pa.

C. F. HEVERLY.

OVERTON, PA., Oct. 5, 1885.

ERRATA.

Page 14, 24th line, " 1858 " should read 1838.

" 15, 8th " insert " or " before the word at.

" 15, 19th " " Kemt " should read Kent.

" 15, 27th " " Hadens " should read Havens.

" 49, 26th " " slowly " should read closely.

" 55, 5th " " brandy " should read board.

" 67, 4th " " Eldrad " should read Eldad.

" 74, 7th " " 1834 " should read Feb., 1836.

" 78, 9th " " Simon " should read Harry.

" 120, 3d " " continued " should read continue.

" 152, in chorus, " how " should read holy.

" 153, last stanza after the line ending in scamper, add

> " His bosom burned, when there he learned
> That he had caught a panther."

" " 169 " should be 165.

" 174, 22d line, " Cramner " should read Cranmer.

" 176, 9th " " Burman's " should read Bowman's.

" 180, 11th " Wm. T. Telford should read Wm. H. Telford.

" 186, 1st " " entered " should read enlisted.

" 186, 10th " " July 2 " should read July 22.

" 197, 11th " " Corporal " should read Co. D.

MONROE.

POSITION AND EXTENT.

*Monroe** is situated in the south-central part of the county, the township of Towanda forming its boundary on the north, Asylum on the east, Albany on the south-east, Overton on the south-west, and Barclay and Franklin on the west. Its general shape is triangular, the southern half of the township gradually narrowing to a point between Overton and Albany. The township comprises an area of about thirty-five square miles, and is centrally distant from the county seat six miles, with which place it is connected with the Barclay, and State Line & Sullivan railroads, which effect their junction in the village of Monroeton.

SURFACE AND DRAINAGE.

The surface is broken, and mountainous in the southern and south-western part, which is traversed by a spur of the Alleghany system. The general slope of the township is from south-west to north-east. The greatest altitude is 1900 feet, while Monroeton depot is only 756 feet above tide water. The township is well watered by the Towanda creek, the Schrader, the South Branch, and numerous minor streams.

*We conjecture, as the township was set off in the height of President Monroe's popularity, that it is so called in his honor.

The main stream enters the north-west corner of the township, then bends to the north-east, and again to the south-east, and finally above Monroe village, makes a third graceful curve and takes a north-easterly course, passing out of the township, midway between the extremes of its northern bound. The South Branch enters the township from the south, and flows almost due north-west, until it mingles its waters with the more noble stream at Monroeton. The Schrader strikes the township a mile south of the Towanda creek, and taking an easterly course, after a mile, turns to the north and falls into the main stream at Greenwood. On either side of the South Branch the mountains are steep, but gradually lower toward its mouth, and the valley widens into broad, fertile flats.

SOIL AND PRODUCTS.

The soil is highly productive, even on the highlands, and is well adapted for growing the cereals. The southern and eastern portion of the township consists of the *Catkskill red soil*, and the north and western portion of the *Chemung*, both of which contain about the same producing qualities. *Iron ore* and *coal* are found in the mountains, but not in paying quantities.

Agriculture is the principal business of the people. Especial attention is given to the growing of the cereals. Dairying and stock-raising are carried on successfully but not extensively. *Manufacturing* is an important industry, and *lumbering*, which was the main business of the people for nearly half a century, is now almost a thing of the past.

The north-eastern part of the township contains the most fine farms, and Liberty Corners district ranks as one of the foremost farming localities in the county.

THE PEOPLE

Are largely scions of the hardy and intelligent pioneers, who settled the township nearly a century ago, and are a hospitable, industrious, patriotic and progressive class of citizens. The husbandmen have a commendable pride in their neat farms which are well equipped with labor-saving machinery of modern invention. Their stock is good, and many herds contain the Jerseys and Durhams. The farms are not too large, but are well conducted; and nearly two-thirds of the whole township is under a state of cultivation. Monroe township and borough have a population of about 2000 persons. In 1880 their population was 1769; in 1870, 1514; and in 1820, about 200, or one-tenth of their population now.

ORGANIZATION.

" At a Court of General Quarter Sessions of the Peace held at *Meansville*, in and for said county, on Monday the sixth day of December, A. D. 1819, before the Honorable Edward Herrick, President, and John McKean and Jonathan Stevens, Esquires, Judges of the same Court, upon the petition of sundry inhabitants of Towanda township, setting forth, that they labor under great inconveniences, on account of the dividing lines of Towanda and Burlington townships, of the vast territory of Towanda township, and praying the Court to appoint proper persons

4

to view and lay a new township out of the townships of.
Towanda and Burlington; the Court, upon due consideration had of the premises, do order and appoint Samuel Mc-
Kean, Harry Spalding, and Abner C. Rockwell to enquire
into the propriety of granting the prayer of the petitioners.
And it shall be the duty of the Commissioners or any two
of them to make a plot or draft of the sections which
are prayed for to be set off, and erected into a new township,
the consequent alteration of lines together with the present
lines of the said new township, all of which they or any two
of them shall report to the next Court of Quarter Sessions,
together with their opinion of the same. May sessions,
1820, the viewers report, to wit: 'We the sub-
scribers, Commissioners appointed agreeably to the above
rule for the purpose therein mentioned, having met on the
subject and investigated the premises, do report as follows:
That in our opinion it would be for the convenience of
the public to set off a new township from the townships of
Towanda and Burlington, beginning at the south-west corner
of Ulster, thence south to the north-east corner of Franklin;
thence east to the Towanda creek; thence down said creek,
according to the various original courses thereof to the Susquehanna river; thence up said river to the courses thereof
to the south line of Ulster township; thence south 59° west
on said line of Ulster township to the place of beginning.
"'Witness our hands the 10th day of May, 1820.
                "'HARRY SPALDING,
                "'A. C. ROCKWELL.'

" The report was read and confirmed *nisi* at September sessions ; and now to wit : September sessions, 1821, was read and finally confirmed and ordered to be entered of record."

The territory included within the bounds above named was to be Towanda, and the remainder of what was Towanda township to constitute Monroe. The original township was much larger than now, several strips having been taken off and added to other townships. However, in 1873 a narrow piece was taken from Overton and Barclay and given to Monroe.

ORIGINAL TERRITORY.

The town includes, in part, the Susquehanna Company's grant of " Bachelor's Adventure," " Bortle's Pitch," " Blooming Dale," and other townships. On the records of the Company are the following entries : " Pursuant to a vote of the Susquehanna Company to lay out townships to the proprietors of the said Susquehanna purchase, Elisha Tracy and Joseph Kingsbury appearing as agents for the number of twenty-five whole share proprietors, with the taxes paid agreeably to the votes of said Company, therefore said Elisha Tracy and Joseph Kingsbury having surveyed a township of land on said purchase on the waters of Towanda, beginning at the south-west corner of Claverack ; thence north 31° west, 280 chains ; thence south 80° west, 480 chains ; thence south 31° east, 366 chains : thence south, 83° west, to the south-west corner of Bortle's grant, it being 380 chains ; thence north 10° east, 166½ chains to north-west corner of said Bortle's grant ; thence north 70° east

25 chains to the first mentioned bound, and to contain 17,-800 acres, including six or seven pitches of 300 acres each.

" The above survey of a township known by the name of ' Bachelor's Adventure,' is accepted and approved of, to belong to the said Elisha Tracy and Joseph Kingsbury and their associates, to be divided into fifty-three equal shares and six half-share pitches.

" Given under our hands and seals, at Tioga, the 6th day of December, 1794.

Commissioners, { JOHN FRANKLIN,
SIMON SPALDING,
PETER LOOP, Jr."

Under date of Jan. 3, 1800, Joseph Kingsbury sells to Levi Thayer, Elias Saterlee, and Comfort A. Carpenter certain half-lots of land in Bachelor's Adventure adjoining west on Claverack and east on Fullersville, on Towanda creek (the part included in Monroe), which have two roads running through them, one north and south and the other east and west, with a good grist-mill and saw-mill on the same, and six or seven settlers.

The survey of Capt. John Bortle's pitch began " near a sugar house on the northerly side of Towanda creek," and bounded on the north by the south-west line of Claverack, and contained 1500 acres.

The Pennsylvania owners were the Asylum Company and Joseph Priestly, of Northumberland. A part of the Holland Company's purchase extended into this township. This company, which was composed of the same individuals that formed the company which figured so largely in the settlement of western New York, owned thirty tracts of land in Bradford county, which is in Albany, Monroe, and Asylum townships. William Ward, Esq., was the agent for the company in Pennsylvania, and afterwards bought the residue of their lands in Bradford county.

The lands lying on the Towanda creek were originally surveyed in 1785–6 by Jos. J. Wallace, Deputy Surveyor for the State.

THE ABORIGINES.

But few evidences of the Red Man's footprints and skill remained when the first settlers came to this locality. He had paths traversing the township, but did not stop more than to engage in the hunt and fish. In a cavern in the rocks, on the mountain back of Mr. Kellogg's, were found by the Northrups a quantity of clam shells, earthern pottery-ware and black lead crucibles, supposed to have been carried there by the Indians. It was quite certain that the pots had been used, but for what kind of ore could not be ascertained. Similar remains were found up the Schrader, and not far from them, near a deer lick, an earthen pot with a bulge in the middle and having a capacity of a gallon. Numerous fire beds, arrow and spear heads were discovered on the flats near Mr. Kellogg's. The old hunters found blazed trees along the South Branch, and the Schrader. Following the Schrader from Weston to the " Big Eddy," a mile above the Foot-of-Plane, the path crossed to Elk creek, thence to the Loyal Sock. The path up the South Branch also led to the Loyal Sock.

The main trail passing through the township, followed up the Lycoming creek to the Beaver Dam, at the south-western angle of the county, thence down the Meadows, crossing to the north side of the Towanda creek near East Canton; thence down the creek to near Monroeton, where it branched, one trail leading to *Tawandaemunk* at the mouth of the Towanda creek, and the other to *Oscului* at the mouth of Sugar creek.

EARLY HISTORY.

When Monroe was first visited by white man can never be ascertained. Who he was, or whence he came will be unknown forever. However, bold adventurers were here more than a century ago. Tradition says, that the first family was here before the massacre of Wyoming. *John Neeley* and the *Pladnor* family are thought to have been here before 1780. Others are mentioned before the *pioneers* proper came, but it must be remembered that it is to those that came with their families, cleared up the forests and made them to blossom as the rose. and established churches and schools, that shall be attributed all that is noble and heroic in the history of a new country.

Craft says in his general history of Bradford county: " Prior to the Wyoming battle, on the Towanda flats Jacob Bowman had moved near Mr. Fox, while Capt. John Bartles had settled, or at least made a pitch, above them towards Monroeton, and probably John Neeley at Greenwood." Again, in speaking of the flight of the Fox family at about the time of the battle, he says : " Danger from the Indians daily increased, and Mr. Fox determined to take his family to a place of greater safety. John Neeley, an Irishman from Northumberland, had taken possession of the tract of land above Mr. Fox, at Greenwood, and was probably there at this time, and aided Mr. Fox in his emigration."

" Elder Alden " in his writings says : " A family by the name of *Pladnor* removed from Wyoming to within what is now Monroe borough, in 1779, and occupied the flats east of the present village for years. The Pladnors are well remembered by the writer, and it is said of them that they were truly loyal to the Penemites, and opposed to the encroachments of the Connecticut people. But be that as it may, they are said to have brought quantities of beds and other goods with them, that were necessarily abandoned by the hasty flight of the people from the East in their return to their former homes. Mrs. Pladnor associated with the Indians, shot their rifles at a mark, ran foot-races with them, and witnessed their rude life and times, and then in after years was accustomed to relate the stirring incidents to the writer and his young associates, to beguile the indoor hours of a long winter evening. Mrs. Pladnor died in Franklin township in about the year 1835, at the age of 109 years." The Pladnors will again be mentioned.

The *Strickland* family settled on the Cole place at an early day. The first grave at Cole's, as shown by the inscription on the headstone, was that of " Hannah Strickland," whose death occurred January 24th, 1791, at the age of 18 months and 7 days.

THE PIONEERS.

Samuel Cranmer, born in New Jersey, July 14, 1766, started from his native State on horseback, unaccompanied, in the spring of 1789, " to seek a home in the rich and unsettled country of the West." This was before "the day of roads," and he was required to follow the foot-paths across the mountains, reaching the county by the way of Wilkes-Barre. Drifting into what is now Monroe, he found a family by the name of Pladnor on the place now owned by Mrs. Daniel Blackman. Their little log house, with its puncheon floor, stood within the present limits of Monroe borough, on the right bank of the creek, but what would now be the left bank, the stream having changed its course here. Proceeding up the creek Mr. Cranmer examined the broad and fruitful flats between Masontown and Monroe village, and concluded to settle thereon. Accordingly he returned to Pladnor's, made arrangements for his board, and at once began clearing away the thorn trees and other timbers that grew along the creek. This first clearing was about a quarter of a mile below Salisbury's mills, on property of now Mr. Cranmer's great-grandson, M A. Cranmer, and about a hundred rods south-east of his residence. Mr. Cranmer put his fallow of some two or three acres out to corn, when provisions with the Pladners becoming scarce, he returned to New Jersey.

Soon after arriving in the new country Mr. Cranmer met with an accident that caused him much pain and privation. Every morning in going to his work he was required to cross the creek in a dug-out. He had taken off his shoes and placed them in the bottom of his craft, and was making his crossing as usual, when through some mishap the canoe turned over and his shoes were lost. Another pair could not be procured, and he must go bare-footed until he returned to the East. His feet became sore and filled with thorns, and though he extracted what he could, upon reaching home his wife took out fourteen more. In the fall, Mr. Cranmer returned and harvested his corn, and in the following spring moved in his family. He built a log house, pioneer style, with a puncheon floor and cob roof, on the second bank of the creek, and about thirty rods from it. His clearing laid between his house and the creek. "Here, alone in the wilds, lived Mr. Cranmer and his family, with only the Pladnors for their neighbors." At the mouth of the creek were the Meanses, Foxes, and Bowmans, who made up the entire circle of acquaintances in the wilderness. The country was a wild and dreary prospect, inhabited by the panther and bear. Gray wolves were without number, and broke the midnight stillness by music that was horrifying to the ear. Deer and elk were plentiful, and the creeks swarmed with trout and other fishes. Mills had not yet been established in the county, and there were too few settlers and too little grain to go with boats to Wilkes-Barre, the nearest milling point. Accordingly the Indian's invention, the mortar and pestle, was resorted to. This rude mill, if, indeed, we might call it such, consisted of a dressed stone to be used in the hand as a pounder, and the end of a stump, or piece of log hollowed by burning, to contain the grain.

It was unsafe to venture far into the wilderness without a gun, and sheep, hogs and calves had to be confined in log pens at night to be kept from destruction by panthers, bears and wolves. And though Mr. Cranmer's surroundings were most gloomy and his hardships and inconveniences many, he was equal to the test of pioneer times. After making the wilds of Monroe his home, he gave his time, diligently, in clearing up the farm which he occupied until the time of his death—the same lying partly in and partly out of the borough of Monroe, and yet held by his descendants.

Mr. Cranmer was a devoted and consistent member of the Presbyterian church for many years. Long before the church was established at Monroeton, he was a member at Wysox, and would cross the river on horseback. He hated contention and was naturally a pacificator of men, doing all in his power to satisfy the differences of his neighbors. He was endowed with a big heart, and would never say *no* to his friends, when asked for aid in the battle of life. He was a man of great industry, and was always up before the sun. He never gained the displeasure of his neighbors in word or deed, but on the contrary, " all were his friends."

Samuel Cranmer united in marriage with Miss Hannah Miller in about 1787. The fruits of this union were :

Josiah, born April 2, 1788 ;
Elizabeth, born Aug. 3, 1790 ;
Jedidiah, born Sept. 9, 1795 ;
John, born Jan. 21, 1798 ;
Mary, born April 4, 1800 ;
Noadiah, born Aug. 22, 1802 ;
Samuel, born Oct. 5, 1804

" Hannah Miller," who was born June 6, 1768, died March 26, 1807. Mr. Cranmer again married *Miss Sarah Hubbel*, who bore him—

Ashbel L., born Jan. 6, 1809;

Enoch H., born Jan. 22, 1813.

Mr. Cranmer died May 17, 1845, and his wife, "Sarah," who was born Feb. 15, 1769, died Aug. 22, 1854.

Josiah married *Electa Fowler*, daughter of Jonathan Fowler; gave his life to farming and died upon the place now occupied by Wilson Decker (Asylum).

Elizabeth married John Brown and moved to Cortland Co., N. Y., where she died.

Jedidiah learned the trade of a blacksmith, worked at it and subsequently moved to Franklin, where he spent the residue of his days.

John married Sally Steel. He had a farm in Towanda township and occupied it until the time of his demise.

Mary never married. She lived with her brother Ashbel L., with whom she died.

Noadiah married Claracy Gould. He was a farmer and lived on Hollon Hill, upon the place now occupied by the widow Stevens, where he died.

Samuel married Nancy Northrup, followed farming and died upon the place now occupied by his son, Edward J.

Ashbel L. married Miss Mary Griggs, daughter of Joseph and Mary Mason Griggs. The early part of his life was spent in farming and lumbering. Upon reaching his majority he was elected to the office of Constable, and continued to hold the same office for three and one-half years. The duties connected with this office, Mr. Cranmer says: "Took my whole time, but taught me many practical lessons, which proved invaluable in after life." For a number of years he then gave his attention to lumbering and farming. In 1840 he was elected Justice of the Peace, and continued to serve for ten years. In 1845 he was elected County Commissioner and filled the office with credit for a term of three years. During his term of office the present Court House was built—1847-'48. In 1851 Mr. Cranmer and Joseph Smith built the present covered bridge spanning the creek at Monroeton. In 1852 he built the canal aqueduct at the mouth of Sugar creek. In December, 1853, he engaged in the mercantile business at Monroeton, and continued in the same up to 1873. However, through all these vicissitudes in business, he conducted farming in a successful manner. Through industry, careful management, and good judgment, Mr. Cranmer has earned a fine fortune and now enjoys himself in retirement at his pleasant home in Monroeton, only giving his attention to his own private business. Mr. Cranmer has always been recognized as a man of fine judgment and is yet in possession of a clear intellect, and accurate memory. His two sons, Albert G. and Bernard A., have followed him as successful business men.

Enoch H. married Miss Permelia Griggs, sister of Mrs. A. L. Cranmer, and in the first years of his married life engaged in farming. In 1858 he and S. W. Alden entered the ministry at about the same time. He was a man of ability, and was a member of the M. E. Conference for many years, four of which were spent as Presiding Elder of the Troy district. During the last three or four years of his life he had a superannuated relation with the church. He was universally known as " Elder Cranmer." His demise occurred Oct. 7, 1880, and that of his wife, Oct. 7, 1881.

Samuel Cranmer returned to the East with most glowing accounts of " the West," which was the means of soon inducing his father, brothers and others hither.

John and Stephen Cranmer came to the township in 1790 or '91, from Sussex county, N. J., and their father, *Noadiah Cranmer*, came with them, at about the same time.

John located on land adjoining his brother Samuel's on the east, and began clearing up a farm which lies mainly within the borough limits. Here he died May 10, 1810, at the age of 51 years, and his remains were sepulchred at Cole's. His wife, " Ketura," survived him many years, living to be a very old lady. She died March 23, 1853, aged 93 years. and her body lies beside that of her husband at Cole's.

John Cranmer was a brigade wagonmaster in the Revolutionary war. His children were :

Sally, who married John E. Kemt and lived in Smithfield ; *Daniel ;*

Calvin located in Smithfield and married Miss Almira J. Hartman, a daughter of Coonrod Hartman, a Hessian, who was pressed into the service of the British, but upon the capture of Burgoyne espoused the American cause.

Luther migrated to the West and died there.

Beckie married a Mr. Dalton, of Wysox.

Catharine married Harvey Hadens, of Springfield.

Neoma married Mark Lyon, and subsequently Frederick Schrader, of western Bradford.

Stephen Cranmer located near the railroad crossing, on the west side of the public road, on property now owned by George Overton. He was a weaver by occupation, and a cripple with hip disease. On a plain gray-stone which marks his resting-place at Cole's, is the following inscription : " Here lies Stephen Cranmer, who died Jan. 29, 1792, and his wife, Nancy, who died Jan. 24, 1792."

Mr. Cranmer was born Oct. 6, 1756, and his wife in 1763. They had two sons, *Stephen* and *Dyer*. The former settled in Rome, Bradford county, and the latter in the " Empire State."

Noadiah Cranmer, born in New Jersey, Aug. 26, 1736, located on lands east of those of his son John's, now included in the " Hinman property." But soon after his arrival in the " Keystone State," his wife, Catharine, died—Nov. 2, 1793, and not long thereafter he went to live with his son, Samuel, with whom he died Feb. 14, 1829.

Usual Carter, a warm friend of Samuel Cranmer, came to the wilds of Monroe soon after (before 1796), and from the same place as the latter. He located on lands now included within the borough limits, and built his house near where the residence of H. C. Tracy now is. He dug a well near his house, from which water is yet drawn. For seven years he and Mr. Cranmer labored together, neither keeping an account. After about twenty-five years' residence in the township Carter sold out, and went West with the most of the family. A son, Moses Carter, remained and died in the township. He was the father of " Chet " and Ezra Carter, the last named being at present a resident of Monroe.

The Carter family were especially noted for their mirthfu
qualities and in playing practical jokes upon themselves and
others. The following is a specimen : " Mr. Usual Carter,
a thick-set, heavy man, a regular pioneer, hardy and healthy,
had a large family of sons and daughters that were all full
of frontier enterprise and fun. They had their ' bough house,'
as it was called, and the pigeon bed with all of the fixtures
for gun, net, or other modes of trapping and obtaining the
game. All of these fixtures being situated near their residence, the boys were not unfrequently annoyed when about
to make a good shot, by the sudden appearance of the old
'Squire right in the midst of them, claiming by right of
seniority, or of out-ranking them, the gun and the shot and
fun, and all, after the long painstaking of the boys to induce
the game to come down upon the desired locality. This
not only annoyed but actually exasperated the young Car-
ters, so as to induce them to adopt at once measures of re-
dress as well as of relief. At evening the old Queen's-arms
musket, carrying one and a-half ounce ball, was duly charged,
loaded, filled, and stuffed with all of the powder and shot,
that any of them dare stand within four rods of when discharged, and everything made ready for the morning sports.
At early dawn the pigeons were flying more abundantly
than usual, stopping a moment in this dry tree and then on
that one, all the time appronching nearer in their flights to
that baiting bed, where so often they had heard the fatal reports and barely escaped with their lives. Finally, after
many circuitous gyrations they concluded that the boys were
not in the brush-house, and that they might venture to take

their morning meal. When once a few of them had alighted on the fatal bed the others came in more boldly, until it seemed as if the four quarters of the earth were showering pigeons upon that desirable spot, just because there was such an abundance of them that morning that there was nowhere else for them to breakfast. The old gent looking from the window (a board window) of his house, soon determined to claim his privilege of seniority, and stepping out the back way, with his old broad-brimmed hat in hand, so as to be careful, his boots outside of his tow and linen pants and up to his knees, his heavy body, short legs, and aldermanic rotundity, with his hurried breathing and red face, as he approached the ambush, all gave him quite an interesting appearance at that very desirable moment. Arguments were short, he claimed the gun, reaching his hand for the piece in a way that indicated business on the first floor, and to order, and now. The boys retired on their hands and knees to a safe distance in the rear of the old man and the gun, so as to be out of harm's way, scolding and repining as they went, that 'father is always here when there is a chance to make a good shot; he never lets us do anything,' and all that, while they were anxiously awaiting results some rods distant from the old man's boots and brawny hands, both of which had often been used in debts of admonition due the young scamps. Finally, after a good, cool, deliberate aim, and all was right and ready, the old musket 'took on,' 'broke loose,' 'kindled fire,' 'earthquaked and bellowed.' If the heavens and earth did not pass away the musket did, and so did old Mr. Carter, almost. A huge heap of body and breeches came tumbling end over end back at the boys, sometimes the big hat under him, and sometimes it was on top, but everything was after the boys now in a heterogeneous pile. The boys were frightened, and the old man dead—at least, so he said. After a dozen or twenty oh! oh! oh's, and ' I am killed!' ' I am dying!' 'blast that gun!' the old man told his eldest son to call mother, for 'I am dying!' ' Ude ' the young imp, took a look at the dead pigeons and then at his prostrate father, in some little concern, for the first time in his life, probably. After some little time the father regained his powers so as to be able to vehemently exclaim, 'I am killed! I am dying!' 'Well,' exclaimed Ude,' the mischievous imp of the whole Carter family, ' you are dying like Samson, for you have killed more in your death than in your whole life,' at the same time taking another look at the piles of feathers, wings, legs, feet, heads, and slaughtered pigeons in the direction where the gun had been pointed. The gun was found in due time, all sound ; nothing seemingly could burst or break it. The old man was helped to the house by his wife, where he soon recovered, being about as invulnerable as his gun. The pigeons and pieces of pigeons were picked up, but could not be counted in that mutilated condition. The father was a member of the church and abstained from swearing on this trying occasion. He said grace at the table, while ' Ude ' would run off with the meat plate during the short service. He never interfered with their shots after that."

Peter Edsall and the *Millers, Daniel, Shadrach, Jacob, William,* and *Moses,* all natives of " The Land of Pancakes,"

migrated to Monroe at about the same time as did the Carter family. Edsall had married " Jane Miller," sister of Mrs
Samuel Cranmer. He located on the place now owned and
occupied by Mrs. Wm. Parks. He subsequently deserted
his family and went to Canada.

Mrs. Edsall, who was born Nov. 25, 1770, died in the
township Jan. 1, 1839. A son, *John Edsall*, born Sept. 20,
1803, located upon the place at South Branch, now occupied
by his son's heirs.

Mary married Lebbeus Marcy, of Monroe, and a second
daughter, *Jane*, married Jeremiah Blackman, also a resident
of the township.

Upon the settlement of Albany the Millers went hither,
Daniel being one of the pioneers, and one of the very best
citizens the township ever had.

The *Wilcoxs* came into Monroe in 1798, and with
the Ladds were the pioneers into Albany, in connection with
which township their history is fully given.

The Pladnor Family.—About 1774, a man from New England, named Elisha Wilcox, settled on Thorn Bottom, about
twenty miles from the Pittston settlement, who, in June,
1778, was captured by a band of Indians, detained prisoner,
and compelled to be in the Wyoming battle, soon after
which event he died. He had two children, Stephen and
Nancy. Mrs. Wilcox afterwards married Henry Pladnor
(written Pladnore and Platner), who was without doubt the
first permanent settler in Monroe, migrating hither at a very
early day. When Samuel Cranmer first visited the West,
" the Pladnor place appeared settled for some years—a field

was green with growing rye, crops had been previously grown, and the year before a piece of buckwheat "

After a few years Mr. Pladnor died, and in about 1820 his widow moved into Franklin where she died, it is said, aged 109 years.

Nancy Wilcox married Stephen Strickland, a native of New England, who, as already stated, lived upon the Cole place. His log house, with its cob chimney and huge fireplace, that occupied nearly a whole side of the building, stood on the west side of the public road leading to Towanda, ten rods south of the watering trough, and five rods north-east of Mr. Cole's residence.

When Strickland came here is not known. The first child, " Hannah," was born July 22, 1789, and was buried at Cole's, in 1791. We would venture, however, that he married Nancy Wilcox in about 1788 and made Monroe his home, until he moved to Wysox in about 1798.

Stephen Wilcox settled in Franklin township and afterwards moved West.

Another daughter of Mrs. Pladnor married an Ogden, who for a time lived at Canton.

John Neeley, of Milton, Northumberland county, Pa., purchased the tract of land now occupied by Mrs. Brown and others at Greenwood. It is stated, " that as early as 1787 he came on and had his land surveyed and made arrangements preparatory to settlement. Undertaking to swim a horse across the river at the mouth of Towanda creek, he was drowned in ' Bowman's Eddy.' " His widow, who afterwards married Reese Stevens, came up and occupied the farm. A daughter, Rebecca Neeley, married Harmon Schrader, who for a time occupied the Neeley estate. It finally passed out of the hands of Schrader to the Meanses. Mrs. Neeley came to the township perhaps not far from the year 1800, when the Northumberland people settled at Greenwood.

It should be remembered that Rev. Mr. Craft's statement, in relation to Mr. Neeley's being here at the time of the Revolutionary troubles, is " mere probability."

The Fowlers.—Some of the early settlers of Monroe came to the township under the Connecticut title. Fifty acres were offered as a gratuity to the first settlers. Gordon (" Gurdon ") Fowler and his sons Jonathan and Rogers bought eleven hundred acres, at a dollar per acre, under this title of Reed Brockaway, and accordingly came in and occupied their purchase

In September, 1800, Mr. Fowler started from his home in Tolland, Conn., with two yoke of oxen and a horse in one team, and two horses in another. He crossed the Hudson at Catskill, taking the wagons and horses at several trips. His son, Austin Fowler, Sr., then a boy of thirteen years, was left in charge of the wagon first ferried over, and while the scow was gone for the rest of the train the tide rose about the wagon-wheels, frightening the lad, who then knew nothing of that phenomenon, but supposed a freshet was raising the water in the river and they would all be swept away. From Catskill the party came by the way of Unadilla, finding no bridges over the streams and in places very bad roads. Reaching Milltown, Mr. Fowler left his family with his son, Rogers, who had preceded him into the county, and came on and built a log house in the orchard south of the present residence of W. W. Decker. However, before moving his family from the East, Mr. Fowler and his son, Daniel, had been in "viewing lands," and made a purchase. Upon settling in Monroe, the Fowlers were required to cut their own road up the creek, from where the covered bridge now is. They found a family by the name of *Wheelo* in a little log house about forty rods farther up the creek. The Fowlers had paid for their lands, and after having erected a grist-mill and saw-mill and made other improvements, their titles proved worthless. However, not being daunted by such adverse fortune they repurchased, on long credit, of the " Holland Purchase Company," and this time were more fortunate ; but it required the most stubborn energy and perseverence to bring forth the fruits of husbandry from a wild and densely wooded region, like that of Monroe. After nine years of struggle and privation, incident to the settlement of a new country, "the father, Gurdon Fowler, was called to his eternal rest,—freed from hardship and toil. He was born April 16, 1739 ; died Nov. 11, 1809.

Mr. Fowler descended from an interesting and distinguished family. His great-great-grandfather, William Fowler, arrived at Boston, from London, England, June 26, 1637, in company with Rev. John Davenport, Theophilus Eaton, Peter Pruden, and " others of good character and fortunes." In 1638, in company with Mr. Davenport, he sailed from *Quinnipiac*, or New Haven, where he resided a year or more. He was present at the famous meeting in Mr. Newman's barn, June 4th, 1639, when the peculiar constitution and policy of Mr. Davenport, which afterwards characterized the New Haven Colony, was agreed upon, and subscribed to that agreement. In the spring of 1639 the settlement of Milford had been arranged, and Mr. Fowler was the first named of the trustees. At the first meeting of the Milford Company, he was chosen one of the " Judges." The church was organized in 1639, and he was elected one of the " Seven Pillars." He held various offices in church and state, and was deeply engaged in public improvements, until his death in 1660. His eldest son, Capt. Wm. Fowler, remained at New Haven, married, took the oath of Fidelity and was admitted to the " General Court." His second son, Jonathan, removed from New Haven to Norwich, and thence to Windham, where he died. Jonathan's youngest son, Jonathan, " the Sergeant," was celebrated for his great size and strength, of which wonderful stories are told. He is reported to have been seven feet in height, and to have weighed over 400 pounds. His muscular powers were enormous. He could lift a barrel of cider by the chimes and drink from the bung-hole. He once attacked and killed a bear with a club, having no other weapon at hand, by which feat his fame spread abroad, so that George III., then King of England, had a painting made, the margin bearing the inscription, " Jonathan Fowler, the giant of America, in the act of killing a bear." He had ten children of whom " Gordon " was the eighth.

Gordon was united in marriage with Sarah Rogers, Feb. 15th, 1758, unto whom were born :

Jonathan, March 2, 1759;

Daniel, September 9, 1761 :
Elijah. July 20, 1763 ;
Rogers, July 8, 1766 ;
Asa, May 15. 1769;
Gurdon, April 21, 1772;
Sarah, December 15, 1774.

Dec. 28, 1775, Mr. Fowler married Mary Chapman who bore him—

Polly, March 31, 1777 ;
Hannah, April 7, 1780;
Russell, Sept. 15, 1782 ;
Roxey, July 16, 1786;
Austin, May 3', '1787 ;
Betsey, April 14, 1792.

Jonathan came to Bradford county with his father in September, 1800. He was a soldier of the Revolution, and one of the unfortunates imprisoned in the "Sugar House" at New York. He settled on the place now occupied by Hiram Sweet and soon thereafter built a one and a-half story framed house—one of the very first in Monroe. "Mr. Fowler being sick his wife, Sally, went out of the house one night to procure some leaves or herbs for his use, having a pine torch in her hand. Hearing a noise behind her, she turned and saw a bear standing up on his hind legs, as tall as herself. She ran into the house, and the bear made his supper on fresh pork, killing it himself Bruin, however, was killed in turn the next day." On another occasion, "as ' Aunt Sally' was taking her clothes from the line (the bushes), in the dusk of evening, an immense black bear protruded his ugly snout from the bushes, within a few feet of her, alarming her terribly. · She screamed and the bear merely grunted. And although Mrs. Fowler lived thirty years thereafter, she never recovered from that fright—palpitation and tremulousness following her to her dying day." She died July 14, 1832, aged 69 years and 9 months.

Mr. Fowler's children were—

Jonathan, who grew to manhood and died single ;

Ira, who grew to manhood and died single ;

Nancy, who married Abram Fox, of Monroe ;

Electa, who married Josiah Cranmer, of Monroe ;

Sally, who married Solomon Cole, of Asylum.

Mr. Fowler died December 4, 1834.

Daniel, when a boy, enlisted in the Revolutionary army, and was taken prisoner and kept for some months in the " Sugar House," from which he came out scarcely alive. He rose to the rank of Major, before the close of the war, at twenty years of age. He settled at Hudson, N. Y., where he inaugurated the first school of note, the " City Academy of Hudson." Among his pupils was Martin Van Buren, placed under his care when quite young by Aaron Burr.

Elijah studied medicine and settled in Tyringham, Mass.

Rogers participated in the settlement of Monroe with his father. He located on the place now owned and occupied by Elias Parks. He built a small framed house near a tall hickory tree, on about the same ground as now occupied by Mr Parks' residence. One evening a wind storm blew the tree upon the roof, crushing it over a bed in the upper story, in which Sophia Lawrence was sleeping. The bed-posts kept the debris from falling upon her, and thus saved her life. Mr. Fowler was a carpenter and millwright by occupation, and soon after he came in built the grist-mill and saw mill at Fowlertown. He was a noted Freemason, and a man of prominence in the county. He was elected Colonel of a regiment at the breaking out of the War of 1812, but did not enter the army, as he died soon after, May 12, 1812. He left no family.

Polly married John Fox, of Towanda, and was the mother of John, Miller, and Marvin Fox.

Hannah married Daniel Milier, and moved with her husband to the wilds of Albany, reared a large family and bore her part nobly and well in the struggles incident to pioneer life.

Russell married Sophia Lawrence. For many years he kept a house of entertainment on the place of now Mr. Parks. However, he had first built a little house, near the watering trough, on the same side of the road. After the death of his brother, Rogers, he and Austin secured the mill property, and for years carried on lumbering extensively. One day while the men were busily engaged about the mill yard skidding logs, a panther came, took "Aunt Sopha's" calf out of the pen and carried it to the shade of a large oak tree standing in the yard, where after a hearty dinner of fresh veal, he left the carcass and returned to the mountains undetected. The pen from which the calf was taken, stood not more than five rods from where the men were working.

Fowler brothers owned a distillery and built the mills at Masontown, which they sold to Eliphalet Mason. They took a great interest in public improvements, and church and school matters. They were true pioneers and public benefactors.

"Aunt Sophia," as she was commonly called, was brave, and on several occasions demonstrated rare pluck.

One day, to her great amazement, her door was suddenly bursted open, and a hunter appeared, exhausted and terribly frightened. Inquiring as to " the trouble," he made known in his excited way, that a mammoth bear was close on his heel. Losing no time to look up cowardly hunters, Bruin made for the pig-pen, and was soon embracing a young shoat. Hearing the pig squeal, "Aunt Sophia" grabbed a fire brand and put to the rescue. But despite her burns, Bruin killed the pig and carried it off, the hunter in the meantime remaining in the house. "Nimrod" was hunting on the hillside, where Mr. Parks' orchard now is, when he encountered the bear.

The children of Russell Fowler and Sally Lawrence were :

Sevellon L., who married Mary DuBois, and moved to Missouri, where he died.

Rogers, who married Almeda Morgan, of Wysox, moved West and died at Chicago. He was born on the same day, and in the same house, from which his uncle, Rogers, was buried, which coincidence gave him his name. He went West and engaged extensively in lumbering for some years. He became an enterprising citizen of Chicago, and at the breaking out of the civil war was appointed by Governor Yates Commissary General of the State of Illinois. He proved a valuable officer, and was afterwards commissioned Colonel and sent West. At the close of the war he engaged in railroading in Texas.

Samantha, who married James D. Ridgeway, of Franklin, now resides with sons at Minneapolis.

Ellen M., who married Judge Edward Elwell, resides in Wisconsin.

Hiram, who married Catharine Fields, and subsequently Maria Young, moved West, and died at Green Bay, Wis.

Russell, who resides in Illinois, with his family.

Adeline, who married Lewis G. Kellogg. of Monroe, now residing with her husband at Chicago.

Mr. Fowler died Aug. 22, 1851.

Roxy married Eliphalet Mason, of whose family farther mention will be made.

Austin married Betsy Lawrence, Oct. 10, 1813, and as previously stated, was associated with his brother, Russell, in the milling and lumbering business for years. He located on the place now occupied by his son, Austin, Jr. In his younger days he worked with his brother, Rogers, at his trade, and after his death in 1812, he finished Capt. Harry Spalding's house—the third framed dwelling in Towanda. In his last days Mr. Fowler loved to recite " old-time events," for the entertainment of his friends. He was a well-read man, and took an interest in the education of his children, six of the seven, being teachers. Mr. Fowler united with the Presbyterian church in 1837, and upon the erection of the Presbyterian church edifice at Monroeton, the first in the township, he and his brother, Russell, furnished material for the frame of the same, put it up, and helped to meet the additional expenses in the finishing and furnishing of the church. His biographer says : " He was a faithful and intelligent citizen, a kind neighbor, a loving husband and father, and an exemplary Christian, adorning his profession by a faith that works love and purifies the heart."

Unto Austin Fowler and Betsy Lawrence were born :

Franklin D., Dec. 20, 1814, who married Miss Maria Day, and resides at " Fowlertown " (so named after the Fowlers);

Eliza E., Nov. 25, 1816, never married, and lives with her stepmother upon the homestead ;

Adelia E, Feb. 1, 1819, who married Sandford Plummer, and died Aug. 12, 1877 ;

Gordon M., Aug. 14, 1821, who married Miss Mary Varney, is a surveyor and millwright, and resides in the West ;

William W., June 13, 1824, who married Miss Eliza A. Miller, and is now a prosperous farmer at Liberty Corners. His three sons, Edward F., Jewett C., and Russell R., have proven painstaking, reliable young men, possessed of fine natural abilities, and with an aptness in business.

The first-named is a successful merchant at Monroeton.

Jewett C. is located at Towanda and is chief clerk to the general manager of the State Line & Sullivan Railroad. He learned telegraphy and in 1876 was stationed at New Albany, performing faithfully and carefully all the duties pertaining to the office. By his punctuality in business, and having proven himself a neat and accurate accountant, he was chosen to the responsible place, which he now holds, in June, 1882. In addition to his duties as chief clerk, in April,

1883, he was made train dispatcher and served in that capacity until the road changed hands in May, 1884.

Russell R. was a young man of promise and endearing qualities, but was cut down by the sword of Fate as he was entering a field of usefulness.

Cyrus E., Oct. 10. 1828, never married, died May 17, 1850;

Amanda M, April 6, 1831, who married Samuel McKitrick, and resides in Canada.

"Betsy Lawrence" died May 19, 1846 (born May 31, 1789), and Mr. Fowler afterwards married Mrs. Eliza Wenck, who bore him a son, Clarence Austin, born July 22, 1847, who now occupies the homestead.

Mr. Fowler died May 3, 1875, his widow yet surviving him.

Betsy married Abner C. Rockwell, the first Sheriff of Bradford county. A further notice of the family will be given.

"Mary Chapman," second wife of Gurdon Fowler, was born July 21, 1750, and died July 26, 1832. While yet residing in Connecticut, when visiting her friends Mrs. Fowler would save the seeds of the choicest fruit, and brought them with her to the "new country." She planted them, and the trees, now bearing abundantly in the orchard of W. W. Decker, are the growth of this planting.

The Alden Family.—Timothy Alden came from Tyringham, Berkshire Co., Mass., to Monroe in 1800. The year before he had been in to view the country, and being well pleased with it, sold his property in the East and bought 800 acres of Brockaway under his Connecticut title, paying for it in hard cash.

Mr. Alden moved in with his family in the month of December, with horses and sleighs, having two or more. The party crossed the river at Binghamton, where, at that time, there was but one log house. Mr. Alden had built a little log house, where there was a natural opening, about twenty rods below the stone house on the creek, and moved his family into it. " The wolves and bears were thick all around; and Mr. Alden kept everything, which the wild beasts could carry off at night, in pens. One night a bear came and took a pig which had six little ones, out of a pen six feet high, built of boards standing on ends. Mr. Alden heard the dogs bark, and, getting up, took his gun and shot the bear, but did not kill him However, Bruin released the hog, but she was so badly hurt that she died. The wolves would howl all night, and the family, which had left a pleasant home, were horribly lonesome and homesick enough."

Mr. Alden is described as a man six feet two inches in height, well proportioned commanding and of noble bear- ing. He was firm, benevolent, and possessed of good judg- ment. Though not given to frivolous things, he was fond of humor. For some time he was captain of militia, and hence was generally addressed as " Captain Alden." He was one of the first and most liberal supporters of the Bap- tist church in Monroe, and remained a consistent and faith- ful member until the time of his demise. Mr. Alden was of a distinguished and honorable line of ancestry, being a direct descendant of John Alden of the *Mayflower*.

Among other things, for a change, Mr. Alden enjoyed a hunt. The following is nicely depicted by his son, the " Elder": "On a pleasant leisurely afternoon, in the midst of Indian summer, Capt. Alden and Sheffield Wilcox concluded to take a stroll with dog and guns and get out of the noise of the babies and away from the clangor of the looms and the monstrous noise and humming of spinning wheels, and all that, and have a pleasant hour or two by themselves. When about a mile and a-half east of where the borough now is, and while in their low-toned woodsman chats, slowly walking and hunting but little, they were suddenly aroused to an appreciation of their business by old Carlo, the inevitable attache, of a hunter plunging so unceremoniously into the midst of a flock of wild turkeys, giving the sylvan poultry a most wonderful scare. ' To trees!' was the order of the day for the turkeys, and ' to ambush !' for the men and dog. Carlo and men snugly ensconced in a convenient cluster of bushes, and for a little while all was still. The turkeys being convinced by the prevailing silence that their enemies were gone, began to chirp and call for each other in a language well known to the woodsmen of the times, and not unfrequently taken advantage of. Capt. Alden had acquired a fair knowledge of their vernacular and could imitate their calls so as to almost deceive himself, if possible. He answered them, and they replied and began to assemble in the tree-tops adjacent until two of their number had paid for their credulity with their lives ere they were aware of having been deceived by their language. The rest of their tribe having become more cautious, it was evident

that the sport, there, was up for the time. A fresh chew of
tobacco, some chats, a little merriment over their success,
Carlo let loose and the march resumed rather in a home-
ward direction. It was well on toward sundown, and they
were on the east end of lands now owned by Austin Fowler,
when all of a sudden Carlo gave his unmistakable war-
whoop, signifying that he had business with a bear—immediate, imminent, and pressing—and away they went, dog and
bear and bear and dog, with all of the noise and bustle that
Carlo was accustomed to make on such exciting occasions.
The chase led down the hills and down the ravine (now
known as the To-be-han-nak glen). Mr. Wilcox, leaving
the turkeys with the Captain, made good time in the hot
pursuit, and was not far in the rear of the dog and game.
The game crossed the south branch of the Towanda creek,
about in front of where Samuel Lyons' residence now is, and
held west for higher grounds. When Captain Alden had
got to where Mr. North's factory now stands, two successive
reports from Mr. Wilcox's rifle told of an engagement in
close action, about one hundred rods south, when he made
a halt to audit results. Presently he heard the hunter's welcome note of victory, and knew that the bear had been done
brown, if not black. The turkeys, coats and other impedi-
ments, all deposited on a rock by the well-known spring
near Mr. North's present factory, the Captain starts up to
inspect the mighty game. When about half way up the
battle ground Mr. Wilcox shouted to him to ' bring an axe !
bring an axe !' The axe was procured at Mr. Edsall's and,
unfortunately, it was nearly as dull as a hoe ; at least it was

dull enough to try a woodman's patience severely. The bear had ' treed ' to escape the noise and confusion that Carlo had created in his rear, and from his perch he had been dislodged by the rifle shots, only to lodge as bears are wont to do, in the bifurcation of the tree The blood was dropping upon the forest leaves; Carlo was licking it up as his booty in the hunt ; and the bear—well, he was up there yet. It was, and O ! that dull axe. Uncle ' Sheff' quoted some of the dead languages as they relieved each other in virtually mauling off the butt of that old pine, with now and then a good hearty laugh at the varied scenes and enterprise of the afternoon's sport. The bear they drew headforemost down to the creek (now North's pond) and thence down the creek to Mr. Edsall's spring, the place where the coats and turkeys were left on the rock. Here a light was procured (pine torch) and help being at hand, Bruin was made to part with his hide in true hunter's style.

" At about 10 o'clock in the evening the hunters were telling their adventurous incidents of the afternoon to the collected neighbors and friends before their evening fire, while a smile lit up every face, and every boy wished that he was a man, and the ladies were all glad that such men were made."

Timothy Alden was a blacksmith by occupation and worked at his trade for some time after coming into Monroe. In 1827 he built the stone house yet standing on the place where he settled.

He was required to pay for his land the second time and

to do so, as he expressed it, " hauled logs through the mud during the day, and sawed them at night."

Before his advent into Monroe he had married Lois Wilcox, daughter of Sheffield Wilcox, one of the heroic pioneers into Albany.

Timothy Alden was born Feb. 22, 1770; died Sept. 29, 1859.

" Lois Wilcox " was born Feb. 5, 1773; died Jan. 10, 1851 Their children were—

Adonijah, born about 1792, married a daughter of Rev. M. M. York, of Wysox, and after a few years went West where he died.

Sophronia, born May 9, 1793, married Jared Woodruff, a pioneer in Monroe, and remained in the township until the time of her death, April 8, 1876.

Louisa, born Jan 5, 1797, married Benjamin Coolbaugh, of Monroe, and died in the township July 14, 1846.

Philinda, married Warner Ladd, of Albany, in 1818, lived there for some years, then after her husband's death in 1832, she moved with her family to Monroe where she died. She is buried beside her husband at New Albany.

Permilla, born Dec. 18, 1801, married Jacob Arnout and subsequently Charles Homet. Her death occurred June 4, 1876.

Sylvester William, twin of Sevellon W., was born March 19, 1810, married Frances, daughter of Thomas Wilcox, of Milltown, occupied the homestead until 1856, when he went to Wisconsin and there died in 1882.

Sevellon Wells married Mathena, daughter of Dr. Benoni

Mandeville, Nov. 16th, 1831. When a young man Mr Alden
entered the ministry of the M. E. church. He became one
of the most widely known preachers on the circuit, and for
a time was Presiding Elder. He was a man of much more
than ordinary abilities. He was a great reader and had a
most retentive memory. He was a frequent contributor to
both the local and foreign press. His communications were
full of interest and were a valuable contribution to our local
history, for they supplied many forgotten facts and incidents
of the early times in this section. He was without doubt
better informed about matters pertaining to the early history
of this part of the county than any man living. In this field
of local research he was an industrious gleaner, and it is due
to his exertions that much in our early history has been
preserved.

Mr. Alden preached what he believed, and believed all that
he preached Until the last his faith and doctrines were the
same as when in the active ministry. In the heat of the war
he endured some persecution because of his political opin-
ions, but he always felt and remained loyal to the M. E.
church, even to the day of his death. While attending to
the duties and studies of pastoral work he gained a good acquaintance with Greek and Latin and was at times astonish-
ingly classic, when his associates were least looking for such
attainments. Education was with him a necessary and not
an ornamental accomplishment. His power to acquire an
education was great, and his mental retention scarce ever at
fault when in the prime of life. Some arrogant pretenders
of Greek and Latin were now and then put in immense con-

sternation by being squarely contradicted and successfully, by one that they had supposed entirely destitute of those acquirements.

The following biographical memoranda will be found of interest : " Sevellon W. Alden was converted to God in 1837, and joined the M. E. Church the same year. Was licensed to exhort on July 7, 1838, by Rev. P. E. Brown, the preacher in charge for the time being ; was re-licensed by the quarterly conference at Towanda, Jonas Dodge, P. E., on Aug. 5th, 1838 ; was licensed to preach on the 8th day of June, 1839, by J. H. Wallace, P. E., and the same day recommended to the Genesee annual conference as a suitable person to be received by it for itinerant work ; was received on probation in said conference in 1839 ; was appointed to Sugar Creek circuit with Amos Mansfield and E. H. Cranmer as colleagues, in 1839. On this charge this year there were reported three hundred conversions, and 224 converts joined the M. E. Church. In the regular work, he preached twenty-six times to get round the six weeks' charge. In 1840 he was appointed to Southport circuit, had for a colleague the ever blessed and lamented E. Colson, four and a-half years, and good revivals and great prosperity were the result. Was ordained a Deacon on the 5th day of September, at Dansville, by Bishop Joshua Soule, and by him re-appointed to Southport circuit in 1841. In 1842 he was appointed to Jacksonville station, and had a large revival. In 1843 appointed to Catharine, embracing Catharine, Havana, and Jefferson ; had a powerful work of grace this year at Johnson Settlement and Havana. Having been ordained an

Elder by Bishop Waugh, at Yates, N. Y., in 1844, and in 1845 was appointed to the charge of Tyrone circuit. In 1846 appointed to Geneseo and Groveland charge; in 1847-8 Bath station, where powerful revivals prevailed; in 1848 and '49 to Rochester—third church; in 1850 and '51 to Penfield, two years; in 1852 and '53, Canandaigua station; thence for four succeeding years Presiding Elder of the Troy District; fourteen churches dedicated during the time; thence one year on the Burlington charge, at the end of which he took a superanuated relation; took a location at Rochester, Sept 7, 1862. He was never on a charge without more or less prosperity and conversion under his ministry."

Mrs. Alden, born Feb. 25, 1807, is yet living, though she has been an invalid for some years.

A son, Philo E. Alden, is one of the first civil engineers in the county, late Superintendent of Mines at Bernice, and the present postmaster at Monroeton.

The Northup Family.—Nathan Northrup (mentioned as a merchant), married Sarah Crawford in about 1754, and removed from Connecticut to Sussex county, N. J., thence to the Wyoming Valley, before the "terrible slaughter" so sadly memorable in history. At the time of the massacre Mr. Northrup was at Forty Fort, but went out, took to the woods, and made his escape. For a time he settled at Nanticoke, on the property which afterwards, it is said, became very valuable. "Owing to the unsettled condition of the land titles, he removed to Bradford county with his family," being one of the pioneers.

" He came up the river in a canoe, bringing such effects as the family possessed." He settled on the flats about a mile below where Athens village now is, whence the family separated.

Richard settled in the Genesee country.

John came to Monroe and settled on the Vangorder property.

Nehemiah (generally called " Myer ") remained upon the homestead in Athens, reared a family and died there.

Bijah (called " Bij ") for a time lived upon an island in the Susquehanna, above the mouth of the Towanda creek. He was employed by Wm. Means for many years, and was one of the most noted of the pilots on the Susquehanna. After his brothers moved to " Northrup Hollow," he finally joined them, settling upon the Shultz place, where he spent the residue of his days. His wife was Sylvia Parks, of New York. She bore him a large family of children, but they are now widely scattered.

James also came to Monroe and lived on the Vangorder property for a number of years.

Anna married David Ross, but never lived in Monroe.

After Mr. Northrup's sons moved to Monroe, he came also, and lived with his son, John, with whom he died, Dec. 17, 1804, in the 77th year of his age.

Mrs. Northrup or " Old Mother Northrup," as she was generally known, outlived her husband by many years. She spent most of her time with her son, Nehemiah, of Athens, but was frequently with her other children in Monroe. When something like a hundred years old she was espoused by Alexander Howden, a pensioner for services in the Revolutionary war. The venerable pair, whose united ages would have gone back nearly to the landing of the Pilgrim Fathers, took their bridal tour, staffs in hand, to Sheshequin, hoping for a quiet little wedding. But the magistrate before whom they appeared (Samuel Gore, Esq.) spoiled the anticipated plan, by informing them that a few witnesses were necessary, whereupon he gathered in enough neighbors to make up a general surprise party, and the marriage ceremony was duly performed. Mr. Howden lived after this a dozen years and died in Athens. She survived until March 5, 1837, when she died among her children in Monroe, at the age of 105 years. Mrs. Northrup was active to the last. When past ninety years of age, she would spin eighty knots of yarn per day, and when a century old she would take the floor and dance an old-fashioned step with the agility of a girl in her teens. When past a hundred years old, she would walk from her son's residence in Athens to the home of her children in Monroe, a distance of twenty-two miles. She maintained the vigor of her mental faculties until death silenced her tongue forever.

The Northrups came to Monroe before the year 1800, and *Nehemiah* was a property owner in Athens at or before the year 1795.

John and James, like Bijah, were "watermen," and employes of the Meanses for some years before becoming landowners. John, after having lived upon the Vangorder place for an indefinite period, moved to the Woodruff farm, where he remained until 1816, when he moved his family to "Northrup Hollow" and took up his abode in the "Mathews house," which stood on the identical spot now occupied by Nathan Northrup's residence. He was a stone-cutter by trade, and was induced to the valley of Millstone creek from the fact that the valley and the surrounding mountains abounded in conglomerate rock of the mill-stone kind. Getting out mill-stones became an important industry. A pair of stones brought, when dressed, from $40 to $50, and sold readily to parties from the " Lake country," who would come in and get them. From the large number of those stones, gotten out along the creek, and the valley being the "centre of operations," the stream was called Millstone Run. The Northrups, being well represented in the valley, and the chief men of pioneer enterprise there, their home was dedicated "Northrup Hollow." Mr. Northrup secured Mr. Mathews' hotel property, and purchased lands adjoining, which he cleared up as opportunity would permit. The hotel, being on the line of the old Genesee road, and on the path followed by raftsmen when returning from their trips down the Susquehanna, had a liberal patronage for some years, and not unfrequently, in the spring, was filled to overflowing, as many as fifty stopping in a night for entertainment. The exodus of the Germans from the southern part of the State brought much cash to the proprietor of this " house of entertainment."

After the mill-stone business had ceased, Mr. Northrup gave his attention to lumbering, and erected a mill on his place in 1822, which he operated till the close of his life. He was a good shot and killed many bear, deer and other game, yet he never wasted his time in the woods. Once, as Mr Northrup and his father were getting out mill-stones on the huckleberry mountain, there came up a terrible rain storm, which soon drove them from their cabin to the rocks, where they found better protection. Their dog, which had accompanied them, upon taking new quarters immediately began investigating the premises, and was not long in making a discovery in a cavern not far from them. His lively barking soon brought the tenant out and to the view of the new visitors. Rushing by her company without any apologies, the mistress of the rocks took to a tree not far off. The dog kept the panther at bay, until Mr. Northrup could venture out and quiet matters with his rifle.

John Northrup was united in marriage with Polly, daughter of Henry Tallady, of Wysox, formerly of Catskill, N. Y. Mr Northrup died in 1850, at the age of 88 years, and his wife subsequently, aged about 80 years.

Their children were:

Henry, born June 17, 1801 ;

Nathan, born Jan. 23, 1803 ;

Polly (Mrs. Moratt Merithew), born Nov. 14, 1805 ;

Stephen, born Sept. 1, 1806 ;

John, born March 13, 1810 ;

Weltha (Mrs. John Cox), born Jan 1, 1813.

Of the family, Henry. Nathan and John are living, and within a half-mile of each other, in the quiet and picturesque little valley where their father brought them nearly seventy years ago. They have been very industrious, hard-working men and retain their mental and physical vigor to a remarkable degree. Within three weeks of this writing, Henry has dug a cellar under his house, walled it up (many of the stones weighing from 100 to 200 lbs), and wheeled the stone and dirt excavated, several rods distant. Nathan, two years younger, will shoulder his stone-dressing tools and walk off to his work, like a man in his prime, and do a neat job and day's work, which but few men can excel. He is a fair-sized man while his brothers are more spare, and in their best, would tip the beam at about 140 lbs. avoirdupois.

Nathan and his cousin, William, have been "mighty hunters," and some of their daring adventures and skill with the rifle will soon be in order.

The Northrups are noted for their generous hospitality and true kindness of heart—noble, and worth more than all the superficial polish that can be acquired by a selfish nature. Their opportunities in obtaining an education were very limited, yet their language is remarkably fluent, and correct

James Northrup was a millwright and carpenter by occupation. While living in Monroe he operated Means' sawmill, and in about 1816 built the grist-mill on the same property. He was one of the carpenters upon the old Court House In May, 1821, he moved to Northrup Hollow and settled on the "Weston place." However, Jeremiah Ray had previously squatted upon the property and erected the skeleton of a house. In 1822, Mr. Northrup built the sawmill for his brother, John. He was "a good waterman," and it is said that he and his brothers, John, Nehemiah and Bijah, took, for Wm. Means, the first ark-load of wheat that ever passed down the Susquehanna. His demise occurred in 1824, at the age of 53 years. He was twice married, his first wife being Easter Hollis, of near Buffalo, N. Y., who bore him—

Sally, who married Gates Van Ross, of Albany, N. Y.;

Easter, who married Jacob Ringer, a waterman on the Susquehanna;

Ira, who resides in the West.

His second wife was Althea Tallady, sister of Mrs. John Northrup, unto whom was born—

Nancy, who married Samuel Cranmer, of Monroe;

William, born Dec. 14, 1809, an active citizen of the town for his years;

James, never married; died in Monroe;

Benjamin, a resident of Towanda;

Cemantha, married Wm. Rockwell, of Franklin;

Nathan, died when a young man.

Mrs. Northrup died in 1868-69, at the age of ninety-four years, retaining her faculties to a remarkable degree to the very last.

William, the 'Nimrod of modern times," is as straight and agile as most men of fifty. In compliment of his activity, he remarked—" I can do as much as any of them yet," and we do not doubt the assertion. He is a man of average stature, great nerve, and possessed of an excellent memory. He says: " I never feared the game of the woods, and have killed Bruin in his den and out of it." In 1856 he was the hero of an exploit, that for cool courage was quite a match for Putnam's famous feat of entering the wolf's den, so celebrated in story. A party of thirteen, including Wells Wilcox, Nathan and William Northrup—the " big hunters" of those days—arranged for a bear hunt. A division of the party soon struck Bruin's track, and after having followed him a long distance, he finally took refuge in his den, nearly sixty feet under the rocks. The dogs were sent in to determine his location and test the ground. He growled like a lion, almost, upon being disturbed, and the canines kept their distance. At last the fiery eyeballs of the savage creature could be dimly seen in the distance, and Wells and William aimed their pieces at the glistening objects. After two or three shots apiece, the dogs were sent in and gave encouragements that the balls had taken effect. Yet all was very uncertain, and the beast might only be wounded, and thus made far more desperate. But at last it was concluded that some one should venture into the cave. The opening was narrow, and upon the call for volunteers, several would go in but "their bodies were too large, or their shoulders too broad." At last the feat devolved upon ' William," who was not the smallest man, but the one of most daring. With rifle in hand he crawled in and crept along carefully, not knowing what moment he would receive a stroke from Bruin's powerful paw. But fortunately at the end of the cavern he found the beast dead, a ball having penetrated its brain through the eye. The dog-chains were linked together, and Mr. Northrup having fastened them to the animal's jaw it was drawn out. The bear weighed over 400 pounds, and its flesh was equal to the juiciest and tenderest of pig pork.

—On one New Year's day Mr. Northrup, his brother Ben-

…amin, and cousin, Nathan, followed a bear to his den in the rocks. The cavern was almost perpendicular, at first, for several feet, then turned nearly at right angles. The passage was narrow and difficult to make a retreat in, so " Ben " and Nathan took the hero by the heels, to aid him in his backward movement, if necessary. Reaching the turn in the cavern, which was too narrow for his body to pass through, by means of a short pole he determined the beast's location. Getting his gun nearly parallel with the pole, he fired and killed the animal. By means of a stick with a hook on one end, he succeeded in drawing the bear out.

William has killed as many as fifty bear, a large number of elk, and hundreds of deer. He has killed as many as twenty-one deer in a week, and not unfrequently two at a shot. One of his most notable shots was in killing two deer, and wounding a third, which was also captured. His largest bear weighed between four and five hundred pounds, and measured nine feet from the end of its nose to the extremity of its hind leg. The greatest number of deer which he ever killed in a day was five, and the greatest number of elk, three.

—One night as William was watching a " deer lick " from a platform in a convenient tree, some beast of prey drove away the game several times, but disappeared before morning. The next night William and John Northrup both watched the same spot. As dawn was approaching, they could see some animal creeping along the logs about thirty rods away. William fired and killed it. Upon examination it proved to be some animal, the like of which they had never seen. It was tawny red in color, shorter in the body than a panther and with longer legs and a shorter tail. They concluded it must have been the puma, or American lion, which is seldom found east of the Mississippi.

.—On an August afternoon, many years ago, William and Nathan were watching a " deer lick," when the latter, see-ing a large buck advancing, fired at it. The animal dropped and he supposed it dead. But as he was about to use his hunting-knife, the animal galvanized into life and sprang to his feet. William grabbed the buck by the horns, but had no sooner than done so, when the animal's antlers caught his tough doe-skin pants and almost completely undressed him. However, he hung on, and was carried several rods at a rapid rate, before the frightened animal could dislodge him and make its escape. He frequently clinched a deer and generally got his game. More than once, like Nathan, he has been chased by a bear, and only escaped by taking to his heels. In all of his encounters and adventures, he has escaped uninjured. Nathan's best record was seven deer in a day, five of which were shot without moving out of his tracks, and in another, five elk, all being killed without changing his position.

—As a party was engaged many years ago in peeling bark for Andrew Irvine's tannery, their dogs treed a " cub " nearly a year old. It was determined that young Bruin should be taken alive. A program was arranged accord-ingly. The men were to form in a circle around the tree, with Nathan Northrup and the dogs in the middle, while William Northrup was to climb the chestnut and shake the cub off. William, performing his part successfully, the moment the cub struck the ground Nathan seized it by the back of the neck, and though it made a desperate struggle and scratched severely, he held the young brute till it had been securely tied.

—One day during the huckleberry season, Henry Northrup, his wife and little boy started to the mountain to procure some of its fruit. His dogs came upon an old bear and her four cubs, which treed, while the mother remained at the bottom of the tree to protect her family. Mr. Northrup gave the old bear the first shot, but only wounding her, she escaped. With the four remaining charges he succeeded in killing two of the cubs and wounding the other two. Returning for more ammunition, he easily captured the balance of the quartette.

—Henry and Nathan Northrup were up the creek one day with their father, in search of the proper material for a mill-stone. They found a bear under the rocks and killed it with a grub-hoe, their only weapon.

—Early one morning in the fall of 1818, Henry Northrup saw a large panther chase two deer into the field on the hillside back of his father's house. He at first thought the trio were three deer, and informed his father and Frederick Kissell, who took their guns and tried for a shot. The deer discovering their move, jumped the fence enclosing the field, slowly pursued by an enormous panther. The dogs took after "the terror of the Northern woods," and soon ran him up a tree. Kissell got the first chance, and after his trusty rifle had spoke, the panther had passed to the Indian's mysterious hereafter. The animal was found to measure *eleven and one-half feet* from tip to tip, and was perhaps the largest panther ever killed in Bradford county

William Northrup had driven into the woods with an ox-sled to draw out some shingles, when he found a large cata-mount fast in a trap. Not having any fire-arms with him he undertook to despatch the savage brute with his heavy ox-whip. The infuriated creature sprang at its assailant; and with the heavy trap fast to one of its hind legs, succeed-ed in inflicting some unpleasant scratches on William's face. Seizing a sled-stake, he dealt several lusty blows before he could deaden the furious beast. There are several varieties of wildcats, and the largest and fiercest of the species are formidable antagonists in a hand-to-hand conflict. They fight with the ferocity of a tiger, and, with a diabolical cun-ning, aim at the face of an enemy.

—Henry Northrup, coming home from Muncy on foot, saw where something had been killing sheep. His two dogs soon treed an enormous catamount. Approaching the spot, and having no other weapon he cast a stone at the creature. With a scream of rage, the savage brute sprang for his face. He met it with a kick in the open mouth, which gave it a set-back. The struggle that ensued was a lively one, but finally resulted in the death of the catamount, which showed fight till the very last.

The Northrups practiced " still-hunting " only, as they killed deer and other game for food, and not for mere wanton sport. Their usual method was to build a bough-house near a " deer lick," and when the animal came to take its rations of salt, of which it is passionately fond, it could be shot from the ambush. Sometimes, however, they would build a scaffolding in a convenient tree, near the natural or artificial lick, and there await their opportunity. Rattle-snakes were without number, and it was not an uncommon thing to run on a den of them. The Northrups have killed thousands of these reptiles, and only two years since, William, finding a den, succeeded in killing sixty-five, alone.

The Salisburys.—Many years before the Revolutionary War, Henry Salisbury, a native of London, England, was a student at Edinburgh, Scotland. While there he fell in love with Miss Elizabeth Simpson, a young Scotch lady of wealth and refinement. Their feelings on this tender sub-ject were mutual and they became engaged.

The young lady's parents interposing, for some unknown reason the marriage was stopped, and she taken to America with her father and mother.

Mr. Simpson settled at or near Boston, and though his daughter (the only child) lived a lady, she was not the same interesting child to him that she was before he took her from her *fiance.* Her life was passing in melancholy, and her health was giving way. One day as she was feeling badly, Mr. Simpson invited her and Mrs. Simpson to walk with him down to the wharf to see the ships come in; think-ing that the exercise and various sights would please and benefit her. To her great joy the first person to disembark was Henry Salisbury, and it would be needless to say that there was a happy meeting. The father and mother at once consented to the marriage, after which Mr. Salisbury took up his residence near Boston, lived and reared a family. A son, Henry, married Miss Catharine, daughter of George Head, of Nine Partners, N. Y., and settled at Kinderhook. While residing here his children attended the same school with Martin Van Buren

Mr. Salisbury was a soldier in the Revolutionary war and lost his right arm, with a wound in his left hand, at the surrender of Cornwallis. After the war, he was elected sheriff of Columbia county. Having made a trip to the new country of the West with his brothers-in-law, Benjamin and Alexander Head, he purchased 1000 acres of land, put up a double log house, two and one half stories high, then returned and sold his property at Kinderhook, and started West with his family, as he expressed it—" to better the condition of his children " He migrated when his son Henry was seventeen years old which would make his advent into Monroe in the year 1797. His purchase included the land now held by the Coles, and his house, the largest in the neighborhood, stood near the public road between Samuel Cole's present residence and the watering-trough. Mr. Salisbury is described as " a handsome old gentleman of a sunny disposition, with a fondness for little folks, and a faithful and consistent Methodist." Mrs. Salisbury was also a member of the Methodist church. They died at the homestead in Monroe, and are buried at Cole's, the former living to be over 80 years of age. Their children were—

George, who died before his people migrated from the " Empire State ";

Abigail, who married John Brown, of Kinderhook, and resided there ;

Rhoda, who married Enos Marshall, of Columbia county, N. Y. ;

Elizabeth, who married Job Irish, moved to Bradford county, and died in Smithfield. Irish was a man of natural talents, and became quite noted as a pettifogger ;

Catharine, married Luther Hinman, and died in the West ;

Amy, married Rev. Elisha Cole, and died in Monroe ;

Nancy, married Elisha Wythe, of Towanda ;

Henry, married Miss Catharine, daughter of Maj. James Swartwout, of Clinton, Dutchess Co., N. Y., and for several years resided upon the ancestral estate at Monroeton, but finally removed to " Hollon Hill," where he died Dec. 27, 1845, aged 65 years, 9 months, and 21 days.

Mrs. Salisbury died May 5, 1832, aged 56 years.

Unto Henry and Catharine Salisbury were born :

Hannah, who married John Simpson, of Mauch Chunk, Pa. ;

Catharine, married Joseph Lippencott (deceased), a native of Philadelphia, and for many years an extensive coal dealer at Mauch Chunk ; she now resides with a daughter at Joliet, Ill. ;

Henry S., generally known as " 'Squire Salisbury," married Elizabeth Lippencott, of Mauch Chunk, and for many years occupied the " Decker place," where he died ;

Wealthy M., married David Ridgeway (deceased), and resides upon the Ridgeway estate in Monroe ;

Genette, married Benjamin Coolbaugh, of Monroe ;

Delanson C., married Lizzie Piollet, of Wysox, and is now a resident of the " Turpentine State ";

Orlando N., married Sophia Lyon, of Monroe, and resides in Clinton county, Pa. ;

Jerome S., married Helen Corey, of Kingston, Pa., and died in Monroe. For a number of years he was proprietor of " Salisbury's Mills."

The last named will long be remembered as three of Monroe's most entertaining young men of " years ago." Their songs and stories were listened to by admiring crowds, and in the political campaigns their melodious voices thrilled the people and took them back to " When Old Monroe was Young."

*When Old Monroe was young, the people used to say,
That grog was indispensable in harvest and in hay;
And so with an unsparing hand, the whisky it was flung,
And drunkards by the score were made, when Old Monroe
        was young.

When Old Monroe was young, and Uncle Elisha preached,
The top notch of intemperance by many a one was reached;
And dark the cloud of sorrow o'er many dwellings hung
With deep disgrace and poverty, when Old Monroe was
        young.

----

*In the autumn of 1843, Rev. Elisha Cole announced that he would lecture upon temperance, on a certain evening, in the M. E. church at Monroeton. He had invited Jewell Warford, George Tracy and A. L. Cranmer to be present and participate in the exercise. Going to the store of D. C. & O. N. Salisbury, he requested them to come and sing "Sparkling and Bright," the most popular temperance song at that time. They thought they would give the people something new, and accordingly sat down and composed the above before their uncle left the house, and sang it to him. The exercises that evening were opened with " When Old Monroe was Young," and the young men were encored again and again, so that the lecture was very short, and very much to the discomfort of Mr. Cole. The "twins," as they were commonly called, sang the song to the tune of " When this Old Hat was New," repeating the last line.

When Old Monroe was young, and Rockwell kept the jail,
And John and Harmon, too, were there, in spite of bond or
bail;
They cleared the land about the house, and also on the hill,
For grog and brandy then were free—the county paid the
bill.

When Old Monroe was young, 'Squire Brown, he had a still,
And Alden, too, was not behind: he also had a mill;
Old Hess, he 'tended Alden's mill, and Rowley 'tended
Brown's,
And various other sights were seen—Old Bristol with his
hounds.

When Old Monroe was young, Fowler's still-house was in
prime,
And fights and frolics, frequently, were had in olden time;
Like short-tailed bulls in fly-time, they at each other sprung,
And many a battle there was fought, when Old Monroe was
young.

When Old Monroe was older still, Uncle A., he came to
town,
His shop exceeded all the rest, like Rockwell's and 'Squire
Brown's;
The loafers all assembled then upon the Sabbath day,
And drank the rot to please themselves, and so did Uncle A.

When Old Monroe was older still, Capt. Alden kept the gate,
And all who refused to pay, Sevellon knocked them straight
But now he 'tends another gate, as I will shortly tell,
To guide the sinners on the road to shun the gate of hell.

When Old Monroe was older still, Jo Johnson was the man
Who dared to organize a house upon a decent plan;
He kicked the loafers out of doors with all their drunken
brawl,
And strangers now can find repose whene'er they choose to
call.

William Dougherty, an Irishman, came to Monroe in about 1800 from Northumberland county, Pa., and settled at Greenwood. He kept a house of entertainment, and his "log tavern" stood nearly on the same ground as now occupied by the Greenwood hotel. His place was known as "Dorety's tavern." As early as 1808, or sooner, he and the Schraders built a saw-mill on the present site of Slotery's mill. Dougherty sold his property, after a few years, to Jacob Bowman, who in turn sold to Daniel Gilbert. *James*, a brother of Mr. Dougherty, lived on the George Bowman place.

John Schrader came to Greenwood and settled, where the tannery now is, soon after Dougherty (perhaps as early as 1801–2). He was a Hessian soldier and was captured with others at the battle of Trenton. Soon afterwards, he espoused the American cause and joined Washington's army. At the battle of Brandywine he fought with the noble PULASKI and came near being captured. Three times the "Count" and his legion of horsemen charged the British center before it gave way. Schrader and some thirty others broke through, but the line was immediately closed, thus cutting off the brave thirty from the rest of their troop. Schrader must get out of that or be hung for deserting the British cause. The whole thirty wheeled upon the back of the newly formed line, with hacks and hewings from saber and cutlass. Pulaski, determined to save his men, charged and re-charged and finally rescued Schrader and fifteen of his comrades. However, before the rescue, a red-coat stepped up to Schrader and thrust his bayonet into his hip, and in a few minutes the blood was running over the top of his boot. Mr. Schrader once being asked what he then did, reiterated—"O, mine gut, sir, you eats no more breat in Englant. Mine saber sphlit him to his shoulders. I made two men of him, but they were both deat men." After the war it appears that he settled at Hagerstown, Md., where he married, thence found his way into Northumberland county, Pa., whence he migrated to Bradford county. From the fact of his having settled near the creek which joins the main stream at Greenwood, it was called the "Schrader Branch." After some years, Mr. Schrader was dispossessed of his land, and thereafter resided in different parts of the town till the time of his death at a good old age. He was of much use to his neighbors, in fulling cloth for them. His children were—

John, who died in Monroe ;

Harmon, who married Rebecca Neeley, occupied the Neeley estate for some years, and also died in Monroe ;

Katie, who married a Brown and died at Browntown, Bradford county ;

Betsy ; Polly ; Frederick ; Samuel.

John Wagner, of Northumberland, Pa., located at Weston Station, on the "Weston place," at about the same time that Schrader and others came in, but left the township before 1816. When the "old turnpike" was put through he built the "Wagner bridge" over the stream on which Kipp and Kizer's mills are located, and named after him—the "Wagner branch" of Millstone Run.

John and Benjamin Head (brothers) were among the first settlers at Greenwood. John settled the place now occupied by Mr. Andrus, and set out the orchard yet bearing fruit on that farm. It is stated that Benjamin was killed by lightning, and that John was also once struck by this electric fluid. His garments were spangled with polished steel buttons, every one of which were cut off; the current then passed down his legs, and out the heels of his shoes. He was knocked down by the shock, but received no serious injury.

Daniel Heverly, a native of Lehigh county, Pa., came to Greenwood in 1806, and remained there until 1810, when he and his sons moved into Overton, being the first settlers there.

James Lewis came to Monroe prior to 1806, and settled the Shultz place. When a boy twelve years of age he lived with his parents upon a farm within seven miles of Sunbury, Pa At the time of the French and Indian war, his father moved the family to Sunbury for safety. He and his sons frequently took their chances by going to the farm and working. One night while there they were attacked by a band of Indians, and the father, standing near the port-hole, was shot. James and his brother fled from the house by climbing out of a window. The former took to the woods and was captured, while the latter, taking the main road, reached Sunbury in safety. The Indians on their raid took several prisoners, which they disposed of according to their customs of warfare, save young Lewis and a young man named Wm. Thomas, who were spared. Young Lewis because he was old enough to travel with the captors, and yet so young as not to endanger or injure them. Thomas was reserved to be given to an old squaw to replace a son of hers that had been slain in battle. The prisoners were kindly cared for on their march in captivity, but when young Thomas was adopted by his new mother, she went through a most cere- monious routine. He had been in high spirits during the most of his captivity, but when his new mother stripped him and then greased him all over, following that application with Indian paint and feathers, wampum and blankets, the Indian dance and song, and the full ceremony of making an Indian of him, the young man broke down and wept like a child. He felt as if he could not be an Indian and wear all this attire. The captives were taken to Canada, where after three years they were released, Thomas becoming a white man again and Lewis returning to his native place. He had changed so much that Mrs. Lewis could hardly believe him to be her son. "An incident occurred while he was in cap- tivity that cost him some toil and painstaking in after years, without his realizing the object of his labor. The whole party of Indians that were out on a marauding excursion, numbered from thirty to thirty-five warriors, and was occa- sionally divided into squads for the greater facilitating of plunder, and all the objects of their raid. One party of thir- teen Indians, on their march north, evidently came up the Loyal Sock, and then crossed the "divide" over to the head waters of the Schrader branch, and then traveled down that stream; while the other party of about twenty ascended the Lycoming creek, and then down the Towanda to its mouth, where they crossed the river. Each party was provided with a large bell of wrought iron, which could be used in

keeping the party together, or in assembling them, if scattered by a hunt or accident. They evidently had arranged
to meet somewhere not far north and east of Towanda. The
party with which Mr. Lewis was kept, waited at the place
appointed (perhaps it was on the Abner Hinman farm, as
that was the usual camping-ground for the Red men) for
some days, with considerable anxiety, without any tidings
of the missing division—not even the " tunk " of the notify-
ing bell. When many days had elapsed a solitary Indian
came into camp, diseased and nearly dead of small pox, of
which all the party save himself had died, at their last halt-
ing-place. He told his red brothers in the presence of Mr
Lewis, where the camp of death was made, where the thirteen rifles and all the plunder, the gold and silver and the
" big bell " were hid ; where the two trees came together
on what stream, and all about it, and then died within two
hours after his arrival in camp

Some person or family which they had visited, paid then
severely for their pains by giving them all the small pox
Mr. Lewis, in his close scrutiny of all that was passing
marked well the place of deposit described by the dying
man, and treasured it up in his mind for after years. Now
we have a clue to the inducements that moved Mr. Lewis
to settle on the Schrader branch of the Towanda creek
From the description which he received by the sick Indian
he was firm in the opinion the treasures and spoils were hid
on that branch, not far from the present Greenwood. When
age and infirmity were upon him, Mr. Lewis habitually spent
about two days out of a week up the branch searching for

the articles there concealed by the Indians. But he died without finding the object of his search. In about 1840 when Gen. Henry Naglee, who was employed by the Barclay company in making a survey of the line of their projected railroad, was encamped near *Lamoka*, his cook in taking a stroll found the long-lost "big bell.' But the party knowing nothing of the history of the bell, of course did not search for the plunder. The exact spot of the finding of the bell has not since been identified, and consequently the lost treasures have not been retrieved.*

Mr. Lewis came to the county at an early day, at first settling in Wysox, where he owned land on the Little Wysox, and built what were afterwards known as Hinman's mills. For a time he was in partnership with John Hinman, but sold his interest to him in 1793, and moved to Towanda. After a few years' residence here he moved to the mouth of the Towanda creek and built a double saw-mill, where the grist-mill now is at Hale's, whence he moved into Monroe. After some years upon the Shultz place, Mr. Lewis moved to Greenwood where he died prior to 1830, aged about 80 years. He was a citizen much esteemed. He had a family of four sons and two daughters. *Timothy H.* and *Benjamin* only were residents of the county. Timothy lived at Greenwood the greater part of his life, and kept a hotel, which was carried away by the great flood of 1850. He died in 1871, at the age of 73 years, and is buried at Franklin. His children are—

---

*The story of "the bell" is compiled from Elder Alden's papers, be having known Mr. Lewis well.

James W., merchant at Greenwood;

William S., a prominent physician at Canton;

Benjamin L., butcher at Foot-of-Plane;

Mary D., a resident of Detroit, Mich.

Amos Vincent Mathews was a settler in Monroe on or before 1808. He came up from Northumberland county, and for a short time, it is said, lived in Overton on the Paine place, on the line of the "old Muncy road," as it was sometimes called. He made some improvements, then moved into Monroe, locating on Millstone Run, where Hawes' mill now is. Here he built a log house and furnished accommodations for raftsmen. He also had a blacksmith shop and supplied the people's wants in the line of traps and bells, and in sharpening their tools. He is remembered as a real genius, excelling as a bell-maker, and a man of considerable talent, being of much service to the early settlers.

In 1812 he erected a large cottage-roofed building which he opened as a hotel the same year, the sign being ornamented with masonic emblems. James Northrup was the architect, although the building, which was started on a grand plan, was never completed. Mr. Mathews brought in some fruit trees from Muncy and set them out (the first in the valley), some of which are yet standing and bearing fruit. His house was a favorite stopping-place with raftsmen and proved quite a lucrative business for him. In 1816 he sold his property to John Northrup and moved to West Virginia.

Reed Brockaway was an inhabitant of the township for a short time, as early as 1800. He was a man of ability. The *Luzerne Federalist* of July, 1801, says: "The Fourth of July was celebrated at Wysox by a numerous and respectable company. Wm. Means provided an entertainment, the style and elegance of which reflected great credit on his taste and industry. An oration was delivered by Reed Brockaway. After dinner a number of appropriate toasts were drank."

Abner C. Rockwell, a native of East Windsor, Conn., born May 4, 1783, migrated to Monroe not far from the year 1800. He had left his native State in company with two brothers and a sister. The brothers located in Crawford county, and he and his sister, "Sally," afterwards the wife of Jacob Bowman, 2d, came in to Bradford county and set-tled in the township. Mr. Rockwell came from the same locality as the Fowlers, who, undoubtedly, were the means of inducing him hither. He took up his abode in a log house at the east end of the Monroeton bridge, on the very same ground as now occupied by the Rockwell mansion. For a few years he gave attention to the improvement of his land. Upon the organization of the county in 1812, he took an active part in public matters, and was made the *first Sheriff of Bradford county.* He built a log addition to his house, which during his term of office was used as "a coop" for criminals, and is frequently adverted to as the "old log jail." After three years Mr. Rockwell again re-turned to farming, and gave attention to public improve-ments. He built the original bridge spanning the South Branch at Monroeton, at the time of the making of *the turn-pike.* He erected a framed house and opened it as a hotel, and the building being the largest and best in the town was dedicated the "Beauty of Monroe." Just when the sign was raised is not known, but probably in about 1824. On one side of it was painted the head and shoulders of General Lafayette, the other being ornamented with masonic emblems. In connection with his hotel business, Mr. Rockwell had a distillery, and conducted both for some years. The front part of the " Rockwell hotel " is yet standing and forms the main body of widow Rockwell's residence. Mr Rockwell was a public-spirited man, and donated the ground at Monroeton for school and church purposes. He was a man of considerable ability, sterling integrity, generous and popular, as may be seen from the fact that he was one of the first honored, and entrusted with public office. After having located in Monroe, before becoming Sheriff, he was united in wedlock with Miss Betsy, daughter of Gordon Fowler. Their children were—

Maria, who married Joseph Montanye, of Towanda ;

Zera, who was a farmer in Monroe ;

James Lawrence, born Feb. 15, 1814 ; was associated with Wm. H. H. Brown in the mercantile business at Monroeton for about twenty years. After the dissolution of the firm, he purchased Park's mills, now Rockwell Bridge mills, which he operated until the time of his death—Nov. 21, 1875. He also occupied the ancestral estate, which is now held by his widow and sons ;

William A., who was a resident and merchant of Towanda for a number of years.

Rolland R., who is at present a resident of Cincinnati, Ohio.

Abner Rockwell's death occurred July 29, 1836, and his remains are sepulchred at Cole's, with his compeers of early days.

The Hinman Family.—This family can trace its history back fully two centuries, and among the descendants in Monroe may be found a *fac-simile* of the armorial ensign of one of the Hinman ancestors who was a body-guard to Cromwell. From this time the descendants were scattered over different parts of the globe.

John Hinman, the first of the name as connected with the history of the county, was born at Stratford, Fairfield Co., Conn., Feb. 5, 1748. After the Revolutionary war, he migrated with his family from Woodbury, to Wysox, Bradford county, and was among the first of the pioneers there. Somewhere between 1790 and 1800 he and James Lewis built the first grist-mill, it is said, this side of Wilkes-Barre. Mr. Hinman remained a resident of Wysox up to the time of his death in about 1834 when at the age of four score and six years, he made a trip on horseback to his daughter's in the Genesee country, and died, suddenly, soon after reaching her. His son, Abner C., afterwards occupied his estate.

Hannah Mallory, the wife of John Hinman, was born May 15, 1751, and died March 16, 1806.

Their children were—

Lorena (Mrs. Curtiss), *Sally* (Mrs. Hart), *Eunice* (Mrs. Talmage, subsequently Mrs King), *Martha* (Mrs. Luman Stanley), *Jemima* (Mrs. Mosier), *John B., Charlotte* (Mrs. Sheffield Wilcox), *Abner C., Harriet* (Mrs. Amos York), *James H., Walker M.*

John Burrows Hinman, born Nov. 7, 1780, while yet in his teens, made a trip West with his father. They had only a single horse, and each took his turn in riding. Having picked out a location they returned for the family. In the course of time Mr. Hinman became acquainted with Miss Desire, daughter of Sheffield Wilcox, whom he married July 4, 1804. Upon the settlement of Albany Mr. Hinman took up lands adjoining his brother-in-law, and moved into that township with the first settlers. Here he lived for a few years only, then moved into Monroe, and was residing at Fowlertown in 1809, when Eunice (Widow Young) was born. He was then a resident of Wysox for a short time prior to 1815, in which year he purchased the Noadiah Cranmer property and became a permanent citizen of the township At first he took up his abode in the little log house which had been occupied by Mr. Cranmer, then built a framed house, yet standing back of the foundry and occupied by Mrs. Owen. And though his home was in the heart of what is now Monroeton, Mrs. Young says: "I can remember seeing bears, wolves and deer in numbers, crossing the field in front of our house. Everything around was wild and dreary enough." Mr. Hinman gave his life to the improvement and cultivation of his farm. He was a model husbandman, and kept everything about his barns and place neat and systematic. He was a diligent, intelligent, public-spirited citizen and a Christian gentleman. For many years he was a member of the Presbyterian church, and was one of the first to subscribe, and a most zealous worker in securing funds for the erection of the church at Monroeton. He held many local offices of public trust and was always found careful, fair, and of unquestioned integrity. He was known as "Deacon" Hinman. His useful life was closed March 16, 1865. Mrs. Hinman, born Dec. 1, 1787, died April 7, 1844.

Unto John B. and Desire Hinman were born—

Minerva M., born July 21, 1805, married Eldrad C. Camp, moved West and died;

Abner Curtis, born April 11, 1807, resides in Indiana;

Eunice E., born April 24, 1809, married Edward F. Young and resides in Monrocton;

Sheffield Stanley, born June 18, 1811, married Weltha Langdon, and was one of the earliest and most successful business men of Monroe. In his business years he was ever industrious and frugal, and thereby acquired a handsome little fortune. "He was a liberal contributor to the churches and every public enterprise that helped to build up the place. He was benevolent and ever ready to assist the poor and needy." His death occurred May 22, 1881.

Celestia R. born Sept. 26, 1813, married John Hanson and resides in Monrocton.

John Burrows Mallory, born Feb. 21, 1816, married Frances M. Dudley; was for many years one of the most prominent men of Monrocton. In business he was careful and successful. As a citizen he was public-spirited, a liberal contributor to the Presbyterian church, and did much for the upbuilding of the community. In 1855 he was elected Justice of the Peace and held the office to the day of his death (July 22, 1885), with the exception of a few months. "In the discharge of his official duties he kept in mind the great object of his office—peace." He was a member of the Masonic order for nearly forty years. His biographer said of him at the time of his death: "Surely we can say, 'a good man has fallen.'"

Harriet J., born June 29, 1818, married Dr. Emerson Shattuck, and resides at Hornellsville, N. Y.;

Lorena C., born March 13, 1823, married Joseph B. Smith, of Monroe; died July 9, 1883;

Catharine M., born Oct. 16, 1825, married James H. Phinney, of Towanda;

Mary D., born Sept. 14, 1828, married Dr. D. N. Newton, of Towanda.

Rev. Elisha Cole, born Aug. 15, 1769, came to Monroe in about 1810–11. He was a son of Samuel Cole, who came faom the East to Macedonia in about 1775. His possession in Macedonia covered all the plain from the mountain to the river. On the breaking out of hostilities, Mr. Cole loaded his goods in canoes and passed down the river to Forty Fort for safety. He was present at the time of the battle, but did not go out of the fort. A son, Samuel, and son-in-law participated in the battle and were slain. After the " massacre " the family returned to Connecticut and remained until after the war, then came back and occupied their former possessions. Elisha, who was a tanner and currier by trade and also shoemaker, settled the place now owned by Col. E. J. Ayers. After returning to the Susquehanna he was converted, and identified himself with the M. E. church. On May 4, 1794, he was licensed to exhort by Valentine Cook; and May 5, 1798, he was licensed to preach by Thomas Ware, the presiding elder. He was ordained deacon by Bishop Whatcoat, Sept. 19, 1802; ordained elder by Bishop Hedding, Aug. 21, 1824. June 27, 1798, Mr. Cole was united in marriage with Miss Amy, daughter of Henry Salisbury, of Monroe. Prior to this time he had been a " circuit rider," but was a local preacher thereafter. On Sundays he would go many miles to talk to the people and form classes, when the settlements were yet in their infancy, and hence throughout the county is known as the *pioneer preacher*, and Methodism owes more to him for its establishment and growth in Bradford county, than to any other man.

After coming to the Salisbury place in Monroe, Mr. Cole's house was the preaching place for years, as also the place for the quarterly meetings with all of their concomitants. Here was the nucleus of Methodism in all of this part of the country. Father Cole's large log house and capacious log barn, with a large farm, and large fields of corn, associated with his large heart, soon was found to be a comfortable place for the early itinerant and a Methodist home. In the days of those grand old quarterly meetings, the people would come from twenty miles around, and fully two hundred voices would sing to the tune of " Coronation "—

" All hail the power of Jesus' name !
Let angels prostrate fall."

Father Cole was a man of close analytical powers of mind, and needed only the educational advantages of the present day to have qualified him for the most important positions of the church. " For a number of years Father Cole was the chief preacher on all the Tioga charge and in regions beyond. At one place, it is said that he preached a characteristic discourse from ' the cloud coming up from the sea the bigness of a man's hand.' In treating his subject he said, ' he should, first, philosophize it; second, analogize it; and third, theologize it.' It was a singular sermon, but quite ingenious and not without practical effect," Mr. Cole was called from far and near to preach funeral sermons—when these sad events transpired in the new settlements. As the country developed, the ministry grew, thus relieving him so that he could give more attention to his farm, upon which he spent his closing days. His life was a long and useful one. May his deeds and virtues live on, down the ages! The light of his earthly existence went out forever, April 6, 1852.

"Amy Salisbury" was born March 27, 1777; died April 26, 1851.

Unto Elisha and Amy Cole were born—

Dollie, April 22, 1799; married Frederick Fisher; died May 16, 1865;

Catharine, May 19, 1801; married Isaac P. Lawrence; died Oct. 5, 1848;

Abigail, Aug. 29, 1803; married Midcliff Wilson; died Mar. 12, 1876;

Isabella, June 29, 1805; married John Wilson, a preacher of ability, who for a time resided in Monroe upon the Cole homestead; died July 7, 1849;

Amy, Oct. 2, 1807; married Minor Knapp; resides in Illinois.

Salisbury, Jan. 19, 1810; occupied a part of the homestead; died Feb. 19, 1880;

Samuel, June 15, 1817; occupies a part of the homestead.

Mr. Cole had his little tannery near the watering-trough, on the same side of the road.

Jared Woodruff, born at Barrington, Mass., Aug. 14, 1789, made a trip to the West a-foot and alone in 1812 or '13. With no particular point in view he drifted into Monroe, and after having lived there for a short time, a brother, Urial, came in and they purchased the improvements which had been made by John Northrup. About fifty rods north-east of J. F. Woodruff's present residence, they erected a double log house, and Urial, who was a married man, occupied one part, and Jared the other, keeping, for a time, as is common-ly expressed, "bachelor's hall." He had a cow, and made his own butter by stirring it with a spoon in a crock. Be-coming tired of single-blessedness, Miss Sophronia Alden accepted his hand, and they were joined in the bonds of wedlock March 2, 1814. The young couple, full of hope and ambition, began life under the most trying circum-stances, and though their portion of this world's goods was very limited and their privations many, by toil and courage they overcame all, and proved themselves "victors" in the battle of life. The first year after their marriage they packed the butter which they made from their cow in a barrel (not because the yield was so great, but because they had to prac-tice the utmost economy, and had no smaller vessel), took it to Ithaca and exchanged it for a cake of white sugar, a pound of tea, and some other groceries. The sugar and tea were all they had for a whole year. One year Mr. Wood-ruff had but few products to turn off, his best crop being pumpkins. Drying a lot of these, he took them to Syracuse and exchanged them for salt. " Pumpkin molasses," as it was called, was used to save the butter ; and thorn-apples were gathered and dried for sauce. Fruit was a luxury, and when in its season, Mr. and Mrs. Woodruff would spend an evening with Mr. and Mrs. Rutty on Sugar creek, eat apples, and enjoy themselves in the good old way of the days of long ago. Their trips were usually made on horseback, she occupying the rear seat on the horse with him. It was before the days of the invention of matches, and it was not an uncommon thing for them " to go to the neighbors to borrow fire." Through their frugality, after a few years Mr. Woodruff was able to buy out the interest of his brother, who then moved to Spencer, N. Y. After years of diligence and toil, the forests had been cleared away, and fruitful and luxuriant fields succeeded. But the change had cost a life-time, and justly the closing days of a model man were spent in peace and plenty. Of this worthy character his biographer says : " For thirty-eight years he was a member of the Presbyterian church, and was an elder in that communion at the time of his death. His life was an exemplification in religion, an ornament to society and benefit to the community. His strict integrity, indomitable industry, united with benevolence, rendered him almost invaluable in the church and community. Surely, we can say, ' a good man has met his fate.' " His demise occurred at the homestead, June 9, 1875.

" Sophronia Alden " Woodruff was born at Tyringham, Mass., May 9. 1793 and migrated to Monroe with her father's family in 1800. " For sixty years she was a communicant and supporter of the Presbyterian church, and with her husband rendered valuable aid to the church and its institutions generally." She was a faithful and devoted companion, a kind mother, and bore her part most nobly in the struggles incident to pioneer life. She died April 8, 1876.

The children of Jared and Sophronia Woodruff were—

Corydon, born Dec. 26, 1814; was drowned June 5. 1837;

Philinda, born Nov 6, 1817; married Dr. E. H. Mason;

Phidelia, born Feb. 23, 1820; married Jonas P. Smith; died March 23, 1856;

Jared F., born Jan. 12, 1823; occupies the homestead;

Bernice, born March 29, 1832; married George D. Jackson, of Dushore, Sullivan county, Pa.;

Oscar H., born Feb. 13, 1836; studied dentistry and located at Towanda. He was a young man of much promise, possessed of endearing qualities and a noble Christian nature, but was called to the " Evergreen Shore " in the vigor of manhood and usefulness, Oct. 29, 1865.

The Irvines (originally spelled Irwin).—John Irvine, born in Scotland, emigrated to this country with his parents, and settled near Milton, Northumberland county, Pa, where he owned a farm. During the Revolutionary war, anticipating the move of the British and Indians, Mr, Irvine loaded his goods in canoes and passed down the river with his family to what is now Cumberland county, for safety. While here he died, the family moving back to their old home after the troubles were over—whence we shall follow their migration into Bradford county.

Andrew, son of John Irvine, came to Towanda (then Meansville) in the spring of 1813, built a tannery and was known as " Irvine the tanner." In 1828 he built the first brick house in Towanda, was treasurer of Bradford county from 1824–26. and again from 1830–31. He became a prominent man in the county, but moved to Warren county, Pa., in 1834.

George, a half-brother of Andrew, born in Northumberland county, Pa., March, 1775, had moved his brother to Bradford. and being pleased with the country, and with the other heirs, having been lawed out of his property, concluded to move hither also. He had married (Feb. 19, 1801) Miss Margaret Reed, daughter of Wm. Reed, a soldier of the Revolutionary war, who for seven long years of suffering and doubt, followed Washington's heroic army, at last to victory. In December, 1813, Mr. Irvine, having loaded a lumber wagon with goods and his family, started with a four-horse team for Bradford, coming by the way of Williamsport and Muncy (then Pennsborough), up the Lycoming creek, which he crossed thirty-six times. The first night after arriving in the county, was spent at Spalding's tavern, at Canton ; then coming on down the Towanda creek, he reached Monroe, and took up his residence on the W. W. Decker place, in a log house which had been erected by the Fowlers. He arrived with his family at their new home on the 17th of the month, after dark. He contracted for 200 acres of land under the Asylum Company of which Bartholomew Laporte was sub-agent, and was to pay for the same in yearly payments. In the spring of 1814 he began making improvements, his first clearing being about 80 rods south of George Irvine's present residence, in fields of now Wm. Irvine. He built a hewed log house about three rods east of where George Irvine's residence now is, and moved in his family in June, 1815. He was the first settler between Fowlertown and John Benjamin's in Asylum, a distance of six miles. He was required to cut his own road from the South Br. nch to his possession, but was assisted by his brother, Andrew, and son, John. James Reed, then a lad of but eight years, picked brush and otherwise aided in the work. Their home in the wilderness was a dreary one for some time, as not a neighbor's house was in sight, and the woods being filled with panthers, bears and wolves. The last would come at night to within a short distance of their house, and make the woods ring with their unpleasant music. Sheep and hogs had to be kept in strong pens at night to be secure from these destructive beasts. One day James Reed and his brother, "Sam," had been away to mill, and did not reach home until 9 o'clock at night. The sheep had not been brought in, and they at once started out in search of them. They were found at the foot of the mountain three-quarters of a mile from the house. As James was following them along in the path, all at once they stopped suddenly, and gathered about the young shepherd for protection. He was well aware that some animal was in waiting, and for a moment was not a little frightened. Upon viewing the premises, he saw directly in front of him and his flock, a panther in an attitude ready to spring, and was only awaiting an opportunity. Keeping his eye close upon the beast, he searched the ground with his foot for a club, and having found one, picked it up quickly and cast it at his formidable foe. The hint was sufficient, and the panther ran off through the brush, passing " Sam," who thinking it was one of the sheep, took after it. Luckily, he did not get hold of the animal, not knowing his mistake until his brother related his adventure. It was not an uncommon occurrence to lose a hog or sheep by the wild beasts.

John and James had been huckleberrying, and did not reach home until the fore part of evening When within a short distance of the house the dog chased up some animal, and the boys, anxious to know what it was, followed. The animal treed, and James ran for the gun. Returning, John, whose nerves had been undisturbed, took the gun and succeeded in bringing the panther down ; but had only wounded him. The dog clinched the " terror of the woods," but was soon crushed to the ground. James grasped a club and fought for his faithful canine, until John could again give him the contents of his rifle and end his existence. However, the animal had so fastened his claws and fangs into the dog's body, that he had to be torn from him after death.

Mr. Irvine with the aid of his sons fought the savagery of nature, and in the course of years, hardship and toil, had cleared up a large farm and paid for it. Grain and game were generally plentiful, but once in a great while there would be a scarcity of the former. One season crops were a failure and Mr. Irvine was required to go to Northumberland for a supply of corn and wheat. For some years he gave attention to lumbering and built a mill on his premises on Marcy Run. In the "big flood" the mill was taken away, but another was afterwards built upon the place.

George Irvine was an estimable citizen, quiet and obliging, with a big heart for his poor neighbors. He was a liberal supporter of the churches and schools, and labored generally for the public good. He was of a pacificating nature, and was frequently called to adjust the differences of his friends. As a man he was especially noted for his sterling integrity, and good common sense. Physically he was powerful, but his quiet nature never led him into difficulties. His demise occurred at the homestead, March 23, 1844.

"Margaret Reed," born March 26, 1780, was a faithful companion and a very devout Christian. She was a member of the Presbyterian church for over 73 years, and one of the few that belonged to that denomination when their meetings were held at the old Court House in Towanda. Upon the organization of the class at Monroe, she joined there, and remained faithful and consistent up to her dying day— Feb. 17, 1872.

Unto George and Margaret Irvine were born—

John, Dec. 17, 1801 ; married Martha Arnout, subsequently Patience Merrett; lived in Asylum till 1840, then moved into Wyalusing, where he died Oct. 16, 1881 ;

James Reed, Nov. 22, 1805 ; married Sarah Bull May 16, 1833 ; purchased the place which he now occupies, and began improvements and built a log house thereon in 1829. He cleared up his entire farm, and for forty-nine years was a pilot on the Susquehanna for his father, himself and others. In addition to his own farm, he has helped to clear up two others, besides having engaged in lumbering for some years. Mr. Irvine is a hale old gentleman of remarkable physique and memory. No man living in the county of his age, has a more accurate memory than he, and can tell as much of the history of central Bradford from 1813 forward as he can. He says: " I made my first visit to Towanda in 1814, where there were then but seven houses. These were Wm. Means', Andrew Irvine's, Adam Conley's, Henry Mercur's, Jesse Woodruff's, Simon Spalding's, and Ebenezer Gregory's." Mr. Irvine has many pleasant recollections, which are scattered along through this volume. He has been a useful and enterprising citizen, and is much esteemed by his neighbors. Our wish is, may his youth return to him, that succeeding generations may listen to his tales of when old Monroe was young.

The children of James Reed and Sarah Irvine are :

Elizabeth, who married Hiram Stevens ;

Samuel, who occupies the homestead ;

Sarah Bull Irvine was born June 21, 1810; died July 13. 1885.

Welch Irvine, brother of Andrew and George, born in Cumberland county, Pa., June 15, 1780, was a boat builder by occupation, and followed boating on the West Branch and the Susquehanna for several years. Two brothers having already settled in the county, makes it obvious why he followed. He came into Monroe from Lewisburg, Pa., with his wife and child, in 1814. For awhile he stopped with his brother at Fowlertown, and in the meantime began improvements upon the lands which he had purchased at Liberty

Corners. He erected a hewed log house, and moved his family in sometime in 1815, being required to cut his own road from his brother George's His home was about twenty rods south of Mr. G. C. Irvine's present residence, on the opposite side of the road. Here upon his hundred-acre farm he spent his life in a most industrious manner. The first few years were the most trying, and he was frequently required to work for Mr. Fox, Bowman, or Means to provide the more immediate wants of his family. With the aid of his sons, he cleared up his farm, enjoyed his closing days in plenty, and, after reaching the allotted age of man, his soul took flight and passed to the God who gave it. " Mr. Irvine was a man." He was a faithful member of the M. E. church, and was one of the best read men of his time on the Scriptures. His life was pure, and his virtues and integrity unquestioned.

July 15, 1810, Welch Irvine and Miss Mary M. Kester were united in wedlock. Mrs. Irvine was a most estimable lady, and bore her part well in the scramble for a home in the wilderness. Early in life she became a communicant of the Presbyterian church, but joined the church of her husband in 1839, remaining faithful till the last. This good woman was born Feb. 4, 1793, and departed this life Nov. 16, 1849. Her husband survived her only three months, his demise occurring Feb. 12, 1850.

Their children were—

John B., born June 22, 1813; engaged in the foundry business at Towanda for some years; died Aug. 16, 1860;

George K., born Apr. 18, 1815; migrated to Mississippi over forty years ago, where he still resides;

Guy C., born Aug. 25, 1816; occupies the ancestral estate;

Catharine M., born Nov. 27, 1819; married John White, of Monroe; died Aug. 4, 1841;

James W., born March 6, 1825; located at Liberty Corners, and well-known to the people for years, as postmaster, merchant and farmer;

Maria A., born April 8, 1828; married Harry Benjamin, of Asylum.

John D. Sanders, a native of Maryland, came to Monroe in about 1802–3, and settled the Ridgeway place. He moved into his log cabin before it had either door or windows. A blanket was supplemented for the former, and at night wolves would scratch against it, in the hope of admittance. Mr. Sanders had a large tract of land, erected a mill and engaged in lumbering for a few years, then sold out to Burr Ridgeway and removed West

Daniel Gilbert settled at Greenwood in 1812 or '13. He was a son of Samuel Gilbert, a native of Connecticut, who migrated to Pennsylvania in about 1790, and lived at Plymouth for a short time. At about the time the French began coming to the county, he came also and settled below them, in Asylum. In 1809 or '10, Daniel moved to the George Bowman place and erected (1810) the house and barn yet standing on the premises. From here he removed to Greenwood, where he remained till 1817, then again took up his residence in Towanda township on the Patton place.

He was the father of Nelson Gilbert, well-known to the county, and one of the present Jury Commissioners.

William French, or " Bill French," as he was commonly known, came in from the East as early as 1813, and settled on the hills above Monroeton, near the Franklin line. He was something of a hunter, and in one of his early excursions he found three young animals playing about in a windfall, and not knowing what they were, picked up two of the kittens, when the mother, an animal the like of which he had never seen, pounced down upon him. He stood his ground well, but was required to let one of the kittens go. Upon reaching Absalom Carr's he found out that his kitten was a young panther. After awhile he took the young animal to the East and traded it for bear-traps and other paraphernalia of the hunter.

French afterwards had an adventure with a panther which did not result as profitably to him as the first one did. He struck the track of the animal just before dark, and followed it until darkness had fully set in, when the game took refuge in a tree. It was too dark to aim with certainty, so he took the lock from his gun to strike a fire with the flint, and by accident built the fire over it; the heat took the temper out of the lock, and his design was defeated. He resolved to wait till morning, and then make a new attempt on the game. But Morpheus soon engaged his attention, and he fell asleep, the panther still over his head in the tree. When French awoke the next morning the panther was not to be seen, having decamped during the hunter's sleep.

The Frenches were wont to go with their bags in search

of rattlesnakes. They captured many, thinking that there was a fortune in the enterprise, and took them down the river and disposed of them, however, without realizing their anticipations.

Anthony Vanderpool (originally Vander Poel), a Hollander by birth, came to Bradford county from Kinderhook, Columbia county, N. Y, in about 1790. He was a soldier in the War of the Revolution for three years, and the ancestor of the large family of that name now in the county. His first stopping-place was *Aquaga*, where he remained a year or two, then came to *Durell Creek*, and thence moved into the French settlement and engaged in the employ of that colony. We next find him in Monroe, where he built a small log-mill (referred to as the " tub mill ") on the South Branch. " Fowler's mill " afterwards occupied the same site. After remaining here for four or five years, and being despoiled of the title of his land, he again sought a new field of quietness. For a number of years he lived at Liberty Corners on the Hollon place and formed a considerable settlement there with his sons, and perhaps others. They lived in huts and had cleared a portion of the farm. It is stated that they had a burial upon the place. Again, as early as 1816, we find the family living on " Ellis Hill," having as many as six or seven cabins on the place now known as the " Williams farm." Their settlement was known as " Pool Town," and the hill as " Pool Hill." From here the family scattered, numerous descendants being found in the county, in settlements of their own kind. For a few years Mr. Vanderpool also resided upon the " Goff place," and Wm. Northrup and Wm. Tallady were frequent play-mates of his younger boys He died at Hale's in 1839, it is claimed aged 99 years, and was buried at Ellis Hill. His wife was Elizabeth Johnson. She died in 1837, and is also buried at Ellis Hill Their children were—William, Anthony, Richard, Mary, Peter, Samuel, Lovina (" Vina "), Abraham, Henry, and Eleanor. The last named, Mrs. John Johnson, aged nearly 80 years, is the only one of the family living. William lived to be a centenarian, and all the others to a good age.

The Vanderpools and Johnsons.—Hollanders early settled on the Hudson both above and below Albany, and their names are left to this day among the " Vans." " *The Vanderpool family* settled in the Mohawk valley west of Albany, and were a prominent and somewhat important family in the early history of that section of the country. Judge Vanderpool was of this family, and stood second only to such men as Story, Livingston and Kent ; in fact, his decisions were held in esteem with all the jurists and barristers of the State. Anthony Vanderpool was of this family. There in the valley districts the family were both numerous and influential, and among its members owned and cultivated large real estates, some of which remain in the possession of the lineal families until this day." Martin Van Buren, the eighth President of the United States, was a nephew of Anthony Vanderpool, his mother being a sister.

Sir William Johnson, who bore so prominent a part in the French and Indian war, was given the management of the landed estate of his uncle, Sir Peter Warren, in the Mohawk

valley, upon condition that he would undertake its improvement and settlement. Accepting the offer he established
himself in the valley at Warrensburg, 24 miles from Sche-
nectady. " In addition to the settling and improving of the
country, he embarked in trade with the Indians, whom he
always treated with perfect honesty and justice. This course,
added to his easy but dignified and affable manner, and the
intimacy which he cultivated with them, by accommodating
himself to their manners and sometimes even to their dress,
soon won for him their entire confidence, so that he acquired
an influence over them greater than was ever possessed by
any other white man. He became a master of their language, speaking many of their dialects perfectly, and was
thoroughly acquainted with their peculiar habits, beliefs and
customs. He was adopted by the *Mohawks* as one of their
own tribe, chosen sachem, and named *Wariaghejaghe*, ' he
who has charge of affairs.' " He was the founder of Johns-
town, lived in the style of an old English baron, and exer-
cised the most unbounded hospitality. About 1740 he
married *Catharine Wisenburgh*, a German girl, who died
young, leaving him a widower with three children—à son,
John, knighted in 1765, and two daughters, who married,
respectively, Col. Claus and Col. Guy Johnson. Sir William
never married again. He had for some years many mis-
tresses, both Indian and white, by whom it is said he had
100 children. Mary, or as she is generally called, " Molly"
Brant, the sister of Joseph Brant, the great Mohawk sachem,
whom he took to his house, and with whom he lived hap-
pily till death, is by some termed his wife, but they were

never legally married. He had eight children by her, whom he provided for by his will, in which he calls them his natural children. Not only were his illegitimate children called "Johnson," but tradition says, "because of his high standing among the Indians, they named many of their *papooses* after him." Hence it is seen that the Johnsons coming from the Mohawk valley are either *mongrels* or *full blooded Indians*.

The origin of the two families named in the caption has now been fully defined, and we come to the reason of Mr. Vanderpool's migration to Bradford county. As already stated, it is seen that the Vanderpools were a family of standing and affluence; and that in adjacent territory to them were large fragments of the once powerful Mohawk nation. "The Oneida tribe was a part of the original Mohawk nation, and this tribe had their head centre contiguous to Albany on their east, and Utica in their western association." Now it is easy to see how Anthony Vanderpool became acquainted with Elizabeth Johnson. It is said that he married her because she won his heart by befriending him in time of Indian hostilities; and also, that a pleasant face, though yellow, captivated him, and both becoming environed in love, matrimony was the natural result. This move was decidedly distasteful to the haughty and somewhat aristocratic Dutch family, and hence Anthony (called "Antony") having gained the displeasure of the family was cast off. He came to Bradford county while the Indians were yet here. Mr. Vanderpool is described as a man well-built, about six feet high, with all the characteristics of a "Dutchman," and some of the Indian, resulting from association. He was known as " King Pool" and was a man of no particular faults. Mrs. Vanderpool is remembered as a common-sized woman of dark yellow skin, pleasant countenance, slow of speech and fond of smoking. She was known as " Queen Pool," and the old people do not hesitate in saying that she belonged to the Oneida tribe. The complexion of the children varied, some being lighter than others. They had the characteristics of both the Hollander and Indian. Their language, impure, was strongly of the Dutch accent ; while their dispositions were akin to those of the Indian.

It is stated that the father of " King Pool " came directly from Holland, and lived for a time at Kinderhook.

Isaac Wheeler came to the county with Anthony Vanderpool, and moved from place to place with him. He was the " Wheeler" living on the South Branch when the Fowlers came in. He was a drummer in the Revolutionary war, and drew a pension afterwards. His wife was Eleanor Johnson. In 1822 he moved to Indiana, where he died.

Nicholas Johnson, a brother of " Eleanor Wheeler," also came from Kinderhook to the county between 1797—1800. Others of the name followed ; also *Ambrose Vincent, Henry Cornelius,* and a family by the name of *Heeman.* It is said that Mrs. Heeman and Mrs. Vincent were sisters of Mrs. Vanderpool.

Brown and Roberts.—" The earliest settlers of Monroe found at the confluence of the Towanda creek with the South Branch, two hunters, named respectively Brown and Roberts, snugly ensconced in a strong, well-built log cabin, or house, on the identical spot where the first county jail after-wards found a foundation. Neither of the hunters had any family. Each had a faithful dog and a trusty rifle, and a hunter's habits and constitution. Roberts, upon a time, went away, whether to hunt or for some other purpose, is not known, but he never returned. Some twenty years after-ward a human skeleton and the remains of a rifle were found, overgrown with roots and the accumulations of time, within the ruins of one of the old French cabins, near Laddsburg. Conjecture has it that this was, perhaps, the last of the long missing Roberts. Brown was left with his two famous bear dogs, 'Carlo' and 'Range,' and a never failing heart and rifle, by which to obtain a living for himself and food for the dogs. He was a genial, kind-hearted man; he made war upon the bears, panthers, wolves, elk, and all smaller game as he needed, but lived in peace and friendship with all the new comers to the settlement. When he had an abundance of game he was always ready to divide it all over the settle-ment, which was, in fact, a common custom of those primi-tive times. A fat deer fed every family within reach. Rob-erts after a time ceased to be talked about, and Brown and his dogs were contented and prosperous.

"A change was to occur that interrupted the quiet of the cabin, and the serene happiness of the entire little communi-ty. Brown was taken sick, was sick long, and grew slowly worse for weeks and months, and it was whispered by nearly all that he could not recover. The young men supplied him with the delicacies of the forest and stream, while the chil-dren gathered him berries and fruit; and both young and old seemed to vie with each other in their kindly offices, tendered to the friendly old hunter. The dogs were there by his bedside, except when sent for a short hunt, and they seemed to take an instinctive interest in the affairs of their sick master. Carlo wagged his hearty welcome to all that approached the cabin or bedside of the sick man, and seemed to ask of them to do all that they could for his suffering master. Range was more suspicious, and scrutinized all comers and goers to know if all was right. The Wilcox family had settled (1798) within a. few rods of the hunter's cabin, and young Sheffield Wilcox took his first lessons in woodcraft from the old man before disease fastened upon him.

"The hunter died, and Carlo watched over him. The funeral was duly attended, and Carlo followed the coffin to the grave and saw it let down into its narrow home. The grave was filled up, Carlo refused to leave the place, and it took time to wean him from the grave of his master.

" *The first funeral of Monroe* (that we have any account of) had no blood relatives of the deceased for mourners, but a dog was admired by the sturdy yeomanry for his attachment. Sheffield Wilcox, Jr., inherited the dogs and guns, by the old hunter's directions; and the ' hunter's mantle ' evidently fell, when he bestowed the hunting estate. Range in after years fell in a most terrific conflict with a huge bear, but Bruin fell in the same engagement, for that young hunter with his rifle was there. Carlo, the favorite of all, lived to an advanced age, ' the truest of his kind,' and fought many hard fought battles with the forest game, and often had to be carried home in human arms, being so disabled by the fierce encounters as to be unable to follow his master. Good nursing and kind attention, usually, soon prepared him for another hunt. Mothers, in the evening, were wont to talk their children to sleep, telling them of the early hunter and his dogs, Carlo and Range.

"But alas for poor Roberts! How did he die? Did a poisonous snake bite him so that he died in one short hour? Did he break his leg in that deep wood, so that he could not reach home? Or did bilious colic seize him soon after his noonday lunch, causing him to sink down beneath the leafy canopy, in a hand-to-hand conflict alone with the Fell Monster?

"Nude Nature was his shroud, the winds were his requiem, the insects were his undertakers, and the tall hemlocks waved his spirit away to the immortal hunting grounds. His dog returned, but told nothing. The great day will tell it all. We retrieve more facts than fancies from the obliviousness of the past."

The Hewitts were lumbermen. They came to Monroe before 1813, and had a mill in operation at Masontown for several years, and did quite an extensive business. ' 'Squire Hewitt" was a wide-awake, stirring man, and gave employment to several men He owned at one time what is now known as the Parks place. Dudley, Wheaton, and Gurdon Hewitt were connected with the business. The " 'Squire" failed, and the settlement of his affairs was left to *Gurdon*, who transferred the estate to Eliphalet Mason. Afterwards the Hewitts went to Pine Creek, and engaged in lumbering there. Gurdon became a banker in Owego, and a man of standing. A sister, Eunice, married Wm. Means Jr, and was the mother of J. F. Means, of Towanda. A brother, Calvin, lived in Asylum township.

From 1821 to 1822 Gurdon Hewitt was Treasurer of Bradford county.

Thomas Cox was an early settler and came at about the same time, and, perhaps, with the Northumberlandites. For a time he lived within the limits of Monroeton, then moved to the hills back of the village, in Towanda township, where he died. He married Susan, daughter of Usual Carter. U. M. Cox and Mrs. Nathan Northrop are children, and reside in the township.

Charles Brown came to the township and settled the Philo Mingos place, before 1813. He was a son of Thomas Brown, who settled in Wyalusing in 1783. He owned a large farm, and cleared up a considerable part of it. For a number of years he held the office of Justice of the Peace (we think the first in Monroe), and hence was generally known as " 'Squire Brown." He was counted a shrewd man in his time. He died upon the place and is buried there in the family burial ground.

He married Fanny Gilbert, and had a family of several children, none of whom are residents of the township. *William H. H.* for some years was associated with J. L. Rockwell in the mercantile business at Monroeton. *Aurice* married Joseph Homet. *Burton* and *Byron* reside in Franklin.

Samuel Needham was a resident of Monroe in 1813, and

was assessed as a *mason*. Some of the older inhabitants re-member attending school with his son *Benjamin*, who settled in Mauch Chunk and became a man of some note.

John E. Kent, a blacksmith by occupation, was also a resident of the township in 1813. After having lived in Monroeton for a time he removed to the Kellogg place, and had his house near the junction of Kent Run (so called after him) with the South Branch. Kent is said to have been a skillful workman, naturally bright, with the ability to magnify in telling stories He claimed to have found a vein of coal on the Kellogg mountain, and it is said brought in loads of it upon his back in a basket, and used it in his shop. When making his visits to this spot, he would never allow any one to accompany him. ' Kent's coal mine " has been the subject of much speculation for years. His wife was Sally Cranmer, by whom he had several children. *Orsemus* became a Mormon preacher, and is said to have been killed by lightning. *Omer* went West and became a judge. Kent deserted his family and was never heard of afterwards.

Edsall Carr was an inhabitant of Monroe in 1813. He lived near where Hawes' factory now is, at first, then moved on the hills back of Monroeton. He generally accompanied the hunting parties, and was made the butt of good-natured fun. A daughter of his married Francis French, brother o " Bill." Carr went West in 1821.

Absalom Carr came about the same time as did Edsall Carr, and was no doubt a brother. He was something of a hunter.

Job Irish was an early inhabitant of Monroe. He was

the father of " Jed Irish," who became a man of considerable note in Carbon county, Pa

Amasa Kellogg, born April 18, 1776, at Hillsdale, Col .m-
bia county, N. Y., was a descendant in the fifth generation
of Lieut. Joseph Kellogg, of Hadley, Mass., one of three
Scotch brothers who came to America in 1660. The Kel
logg farm at Hillsdale was settled at an early day. During
the Indian hostilities, a fort had been erected for the protection of the inhabitants. The opening left for the wagons
was so narrow that the gate had to be lifted off its hinges
when the men went out to their work One day while the
men were in the fields, the news came that the Indians were
about to make an attack. Mrs. Kellogg (mother of Amasa)
flew to the gate and was not long in placing it upon its
hinges, though it weighed seven hundred pounds, and usually required the strength of three men. However, miraculous as this feat may seem, it has become historical. In
about 1798 Amasa Kellogg married Miss Eunice Chadwick,
of Lyme, Conn. Having formed an acquaintance with Abner C. Rockwell, while yet residing in the East, the latter,
upon being made Sheriff in 1813, wrote his friend, Kellogg,
a promising letter, which brought him in as a prospector.
Rockwell made him his deputy, but during the summer he
found time enough to go up into Albany and make a possession. In the fall Mr. Kellogg returned for his family.
Loading his effects and family in a lumber wagon, after a
journey of ten days he reached his new home. In some
places he found no roads, and had to ford the creeks many
times. There was not a bridge over the streams from To-

wanda to Albany. His wagon was the first to pass up the South Branch of the Towanda creek, and when he reached Albany in October, 1813, he found only ten families there, and two in Overton. After remaining in Albany for about three years, Mr. Kellogg moved into Monroe and settled the place now occupied by his grandson, W. A. Kellogg. He lived in a double log house which stood where Mr. Kellogg's garden now is. He died with his son, Moses, upon the place, Nov. 30, 1851.

Once upon a time Daniel Kellogg, of Franklin, Luman Kellogg, of Smithfield, and Amasa Kellogg, of Monroe, all early settlers, met. The question arose, were they relatives? Upon tracing their ancestry, it was found that a descendant of each of the original Scotch brothers was represented.

Eunice Chadwick, born May 9, 1777; died April 12, 1844.

The children of Amasa and Eunice Kellogg were—

Almira, born Aug. 21, 1799; married John Heverly and moved to the wilds of Overton in 1816, being the second female there, and a most interesting character in the early days of that town; she died May 18, 1880.

Moses, born March 23, 1801; married Miss Mehitable, daughter of Ebenezer Mason; died May 4, 1864. Before marrying he taught several terms of school in Albany and Monroe. In about 1825 he engaged in lumbering, and pursued that business in connection with farming till the close of his life. For some years he was associated with his brother, Ezra C., then with his sons, who succeeded to his estates. Mr. Kellogg was a man noted for his sterling integrity and honesty. His friends were many, and he was almost continually honored with offices of trust, which were faithfully and ably performed   It has been said of him that " if there was ever an honest Christian man, Moses Kellogg was one."

Unto Moses and Mehitable Kellogg were born—*Myron, Mary, Mathena* (Mrs. Joel Rice), *Lewis G., William A., Charles H., Oliver, Delanson,* and *Clarence.* All are living save Lieutenant Charles H., who died of wounds received in the service.

Mrs. Kellogg was born Oct. 8, 1804 ; died May 19, 1881.

Ezra Chadwick, was born at Hillsdale upon the Kellogg farm, Aug. 14, 1806; married Lovina, daughter of Eleazer Sweet ; died March 12, 1885. His life was an active one, and was spent in farming and lumbering, for many years operating a mill upon his own farm. In 1855 he was chosen County Treasurer and in 1870 County Commissioner, and proved an able and popular officer. Mr. Kellogg was an observing man, possessed of a most retentive memory, and hence knew much of early days, and was one of the most interesting in recounting old-time events. Nothing pleased him more, in his last days, than to tell of the great changes of his life, going back to the time when Monroe, Albany and Overton, all contained less than fifty families. His recollection furnished many connecting links in the local history of this part of the county. In all of his works of life he was a just and upright man, charitable and generous in his spirit, and shared very widely the confidence and respect of the community in which he resided.

The children of Ezra and Lovina Kellogg were—*Brunette*

Mrs. Daniel Blackman), *Ornaldo, Jemima* (Mrs. D. W. Brown), *Morris, Ellen E.* (Mrs. Samuel Irvine), *Bernice* (Mrs. J. V. Rettenburg). *Stella, Amy, Ezra G.*

"Aunt Lovina," as she is commonly known, born March 12, 1813, is a very bright and interesting old lady, enjoying vigorous health. For more than fifty years she was the happy companion of E. C. Kellogg, with whom she celebrated her golden wedding.

Oliver W., born July 27, 1808; when a young man migrated to Texas, married Judith Scratch, and died there in 1884.

Anna, M., born Aug. 28, 1810; married Hiram Baker and lived in Monroe for several years.

Daniel, born Feb. 14, 1813; married Eliza McMicken and resides in Albany.

Amasa Kellogg enlisted in the war of 1812 and went to Danville, where, after a month's absence with the company, peace being declared he returned home.

While Mr. Kellogg was living in Albany, Mrs. Kellogg made a visit to the Heverly settlement, and upon returning n the dusk of evening, as she was going down the Long Hill, saw, as she supposed, a yellow dog approaching her and felt much pleased, thinking that some neighbor was near. But when within a couple of rods of the creature she discovered her mistake, it being a panther. The animal turned out and ran up a tree, and she made the best speed possible for Mr. Luce's, which she reached without being harmed.

George Arnout came from Northumberland county in 1816, and purchased with his son, *Jacob*, the farm generally

known as the ' Salisbury place." Jacob had been in previously and picked out the location. Mr. Arnout worked
at shoemaking, in connection with farming, and is said to
have been a capital workman. He remained upon the farm
until the time of his death. Jacob did not come to the place
to live till a couple of years later. Having married, he built
a two-story hewed log house, moved in, and began improving his lands. He remained upon the place for a few years,
then sold out to Wm. Wilson. Other children of George
Arnout were—*Peter*, who died in Asylum ; *Mark*, who died
in Canton ; *Mary*, who married Harry Benjamin, of Asylum.

Selah Arnout, born July 12, 1768, came in after his brother and located upon the place now occupied by his son's
widow. He bore his part well in the struggles incident to
life in a new country, and died upon the farm which he had
carved out of the wilderness, Jan. 17, 1844. He was twice
married. His first wife, " Prudence Knight," was born Feb.
14, 1773 ; died Oct. 2, 1822. He married for his second wife
the " Widow Cummings." His children were—

George E., born May 4, 1798 ; married Mary Wilcox in
1820 ; died May 17, 1860. Before his marriage he had cleared
a single field and put up a hewed log house on the farm now
occupied by Isaac Robbins. He began single-handed and
without means. At first he met with many misfortunes—
his first cow was drowned, and one of his oxen killed and
the other injured. But he was not disheartened, and through
industry and manly toil his farm was cleared up and paid
for.

"Mary Wilcox" was born Nov. 19, 1796; died July 9, 1868.

Their children were—*George W.*, born Nov 23, 1825; *Emily* (Mrs. Isaac Robbins), born Dec 25, 1826; *Charles B.*, born March 9, 1828; died Aug. 20, 1862.

Samuel, went West when a young man;

Mahala, married Jed Irish and moved to Mauch Chunk;

Hannah, married Clark Cummings, of Monroe;

Susan, married Abraham Orr and moved out of the county;

Cidney, married James Deegan, of Dushore, Sullivan Co.;

Joshua, born Aug. 13, 1813; married Martha Chilson and occupied the homestead, where he died June 26, 1869.

Their children were—*Theodore*, *Mary J.* (Mrs Benjamin North), *George E.*, *Emily H.* (Mrs. Portus Coolbaugh), *Martha M.* (Mrs. Chas. Griswold), *Julia* (Mrs. Hiram Dettrich).

Martha Chilson, or "Aunt Patty," as she is commonly called (born Jan. 2, 1814), is an active old lady, and resides alone upon the homestead.

Simeon Bristol, or "Uncle Sim Bristol," as he was familiarly called we find among the more interesting characters of Monroe not far from 1818. Whence he came is uncertain, but for seven years he claimed to have been among the Seneca Indians and learned their mysteries in the healing art. He is described as a thick-set, well-built man of a genial face, full of fun, enterprise, and pleasant mischief. He was steady, sober, industrious, honest and good-natured, and with all the rest possessed nerve. He was a distiller by occupation, and lived at Fowlertown and operated the distillery for Fowler Brothers. He purchased lands now occupied by Samuel Lyons, and Franklin Fowler, and made some improvements thereon. His home was a log house that stood near where Mr. North's residence now is. He was a bachelor, and took great comfort with his hounds, a number of which he kept for the chase. " His hounds were always ready for a race, and at times would break away from their fastenings and take a race to themselves without Uncle Sim's being present to superintend the hunt. The man that was in luck and killed the deer, was expected to feed the dogs and render the skin to Uncle Sim, reserving to himself the rest of the game, and all was right.

" At length things became dull in the settlement, and needed a change. Something new must be had, that would do to be talked about—something to make a sensation or a stir. All topics had become old, even the seven pair of twins that had been so safely numbered with the populace. Free-man Wilcox had killed his huge panther with a club while he was fighting the dogs. Sheffield Wilcox had robbed a panther's nest of its young, and brought the ' little varmints,' as he called them, and put them down in our door-yard for us to play with. The wolves' den had been invaded, the old one killed and the pups (five or six in number) brought and exhibited to us for an hour, before drawing the bounty ; and even the ferocious bear's lair was not sacred, he having been compelled to yield his cubs or his life, or both, to satisfy the energy and daring of the men of those times. Well, all of these things became old and commonplace and ceased to be talked about, and a sensation was demanded.

" Uncle Sim was equal to the emergency. He planned

and helped to execute the new and daring feat that would give new tone to conversation for a month. It was to capture a live elk and bring him in as a living witness.

" Moses Miller and Sheffield Wilcox, two veterans, were selected as the right and left hand supporters. Forward was the word, and away they went to the deep woods. Once in the herd and the dogs slipped, the fun is fast at once. Those right good old dogs, such as Bose, Bessie, Trim, Tige, Mage, Drive and Brandy—they would now make tramps scarce, and burglars law-abiding citizens. The hunters were so sanguine of success as to have taken the rope with them with which to halter-break and bring in his antlership, after learning him a few things. You may not suppose that the noble elk was dragged down by the dogs and then roped ; not at all. He could not be loaded with dogs enough to down him. The sport had quite a little more of the dangerous about it than the approach of a prostrate and subdued animal. Some sturdy old male elk, with horns spreading from four to six feet, usually makes a dash among the dogs by way of defiance, and to defend the cows and calves that the dogs are barking furiously at, and by this means he draws the whole pack around him at once, allowing the rest of his tri e to make good their escape, if indeed they have escaped the rifles that first broke the notes of surprise in their quiet camp. Sometimes this old patriarch would find more of fight than he bargained for, and get the worst of the conflict all the way through. This is not a pack of untutored wolves that he is defying, but dogs as true as ever drew blood or kissed the babies' cheeks before the homestead fire. They will do all that their masters expect of them, and quit only at the signal of recall.

"The deer when persistently pursued invariably takes to the water. Not so with the elk. He takes to the deepest wilds of the wilderness and the highest peaks of the mountains and to the ledges and cliffs that he is aware of, and proposes to fight it out in that line. If possible, he will perch himself upon the edge of some high, precipitous cliff, with his heels to the edge of the precipice while his antlers guard his front, assisted by now and then a shot from the shoulder with his fore-foot, which comes like an arrow at his assailants, and often with marked success. He has practiced this kind of fencing for many years in his battles with the wolves that have attempted to carry away or eat up the calves of the herd. When in this, his natural fortress, woe be to the luckless inexperienced hound that attempts to pass his rear and get a nip at his heels or a taste of his hams. One of those dexterous kicks is most likely to disintegrate him from both the cliff and the fight all at once ; and if after a fall and tumble of thirty to sixty feet without choice of a spot on which to stop, he ever comes back to the fight again it will be as a wiser dog, if at the cost of being a cripple for life. Nature has given this noble stag another advantage in the contest that is scarcely ever mentioned in the description of the chase. Like the pole-cat and panther the elk can secrete and discharge upon the dogs around him a disheartening fluid that sometimes is of great service to him in holding his enemies at a distance, whether they be dogs or wolves.

"But here he is ; in majesty itself, and the most inviting

specimen of game that has gladdened those hunters' eyes; and now for the capture and securing of the truly noble and worthy prize. The stealthy hunters advance, the dogs, aware of the reinforcements, become more fierce, and the elk, with steady nerve, parries every snap and despises every bark. He is at bay, and in every parry, cut, thrust and kick he leaves no part of his person unguarded. He fights by rule, not heeding the hunters, for they are not barking at him. The stealthy hunters nevertheless advance, one of them taking up his position twenty feet right in front of the quarry, his rifle at the 'ready' covering the game. The other two men have fixed a noose in the middle of the rope, and a man at each end of it, fifteen feet or so apart, and they are carefully approaching his front with their rope extending as far as possible to keep them out of reach of his horns. If he charges, the rifle must kill him; if he makes a lunge, the noose must catch him, and so goes the fight until the noose of the rope is over his head, or has caught safely his horns, or until he gets his head or horns into it. Not a word is spoken until 'There, we have got him!' 'Hold firm!' 'Call off the dogs!' 'Be quick, Uncle Moses, and get your noose on his hind foot!' &c., &c. Right here the stalwart hunter's richest fun just opens in all the plenitude of the excitement. The surges, snorts, rears, lunges, falls, laughs and bumps and tears and thumps that the three men and the elk take (about an even thing), are sports that a blooded, good-natured hunter can but enjoy. It would draw a larger crowd than any circus. The dogs are relieved and the hunters are more than delighted.

"Clothes are a consideration never taken into the account any more than the shins. The fight once open, all is absorbed in passing events. The first intimation of any necessity for a clothing store is when the hunter's wife in good nature reminds him of his approach to nudity. No account is taken of time passing; all is devotion to the hunt, the game and success.

"The elk was brought down the mountain and then down to Greenwood and to where Monroe now is. Wilcox and Miller walked one on each side of him, close up to him. He had become quite domesticated, except he yet remembered how to kick viciously. He was stayed with Uncle Simeon at the still-house, to repair damages, for several days. Then he was moved up South Branch to Albany to be kept by Uncle Sheffield Wilcox. He became a fine pet, but never fully recovered from the bites of the dogs, the bruises and injuries of the fight. He was a fine specimen, but he pined away and died as he had lived, 'game.' This was *the first living elk* captured by our hunters."

After some years Mr. Bristol married a Miss Wilcox, of Franklin, and moved up the Towanda creek, where he died.

Sebra Phillips was also a distiller for the Fowlers at an early day. He was a native of the East. While visiting at Fowlertown he lost his wife, then took up his quarters with "Uncle Sim Bristol." He left after a few years.

—Among the names of those contained in the first assessment of Monroe (1821) is that of *James Crooks*, the pedagogue. He was one of the most noted teachers of his day, and will long be remembered on account of his eccentricities, and rigidness, or perhaps from the power of his "old shoe." He taught at Monroeton, and in many other parts of the county.

William Day, a native of Rhode Island, and carpenter by occupation, resided at Fowlertown till 1825, when he removed.

Abraham Hess, mentioned in the song, "When Old Monroe was Young," was a resident of the township from 1822 to 1824. *Moses Rowley* is the other character mentioned in the same stanza.

John and Norman Stone lived upon the place afterwards owned by Judson Blackman, for a short time before the latter came in.

Solomon Tallady, who was noted for his athletic powers, lived on Millstone Run for a time. He was the father of Wm. Tallady, of Albany.

Daniel Lyon, a native of Oxford, Chenango county, N. Y., born Sept. 22, 1794, found his way into Monroe in 1821. He was a son of Dr. Daniel Lyon, who was drowned when the former was but fourteen years old, leaving a large family. Daniel was the eldest of the sons, and hence the one upon whom the mother most depended for assistance. He had learned the trade of mill-wright and bridge-builder.

Monroe was a densely wooded country, with huge pines and other valuable timbers. Public improvements had begun, and mills were springing up all around. It was just the place for one of Mr. Lyon's occupation, and he was not long in finding it. His mother and the rest of the family came with him and his wife. Mr. Lyon purchased the Bristol place, but lived near Mr. Fowler's some time before moving to his farm. He gave his attention mainly to mill and bridge building. He was one of the first workmen, and learned his trade with Theodore Burr, who is said to have been the originator of arch-bridges. Mr. Lyon built the original arch-bridges at Monroe and Masontown, besides many others in and out of the county. He built a large number of mills, and the first one in Overton. He was a real genius and could do almost anything he undertook. In music he was very talented, and was not only the " chief violinist " of sixty years ago, but could play the fife and flute well. Many a gay dancer, now gray-headed, will remember how he used to enjoy himself with his lady, dressed in home-spun, at the parties in the happy days of long ago, when " Captain Lyon " furnished the music. He was a man held in much esteem by his neighbors. Being quiet, with full control over his temper, and possessed of excellent good common sense, he was a natural leader and counselor of men. For some years he was captain of militia, whence he got the title by which he was generally addressed. He was firm, but pleasant in demeanor, and was endowed with a kind and generous heart. He died upon the homestead in 1849.

He had been united in wedlock with Miss Eliza Lewis, of Tioga, N. Y., who bore him—

Sophia, Feb. 12, 1821, who married O. N. Salisbury ;

Eugenia, Oct. 15, 1822, who married Geo. Smith, of Monroe ;

Eliza, Sept. 4, 1824, who married Wm. B. Dodge, of To-wanda—distinguished as an orthographer ;

Otis P., July 7, 1826, married Loretta Lawrence, moved West and died at St. Louis ;

Samuel, Aug. 14, 1828, married Eliza Dodge, and occupies the ancestral estate ;

Daniel, Sept. 7, 1830, married Ella Salisbury, resides in Iowa :

Theodore B., Sept. 22, 1832, married Eliza Northrup, resides in Monroe ;

Augusta, May 28, 1841, married O. A. Baldwin, of Towanda ; eminent as a vocalist.

Eliza Lewis, born Oct. 17, 1799, died in 1852.

Truxton Lyon, brother of Daniel, came to Monroe in 1821, and was assessed as a " wool-carder," and in the year following to a half-interest in a " fulling-mill," which had been purchased perhaps by his mother, and held for a few years. In the course of time Mr. Lyon went West, made money, became a member of the State Legislature, but lost his life and property in the time of the civil war. He was the father of William Lyon, of Albany. Others of the Lyon family were : *Randolph*, who went to Canada and became famous as a musician ; *Marcus ; Sally* (Mrs. Sherman Havens) ; *Cynthia* (Mrs. Isaac Huyck) ; *Laura* (Mrs. Ross). Mrs. Dr. Lyon, *nee Elizabeth Noble*, was born March 2, 1775, died in 1851, and is buried at Monrocton.

Judson Blackman, born at Peru, Mass., Nov. 30, 1798, removed to Connecticut with his parents, thence to Pipe Creek, N. Y., whence he found his way into Monroe, Bradford county, in 1820 or '21. He had formed an acquaintance with Isaac Lawrence, who was employed by the Fowlers in their fulling factory, and came in through his inducements. In 1821 we find him assessed as a "clothier," and in the next three years succeeding to a one-half interest in a fulling mill and 328 acres of land. In about 1825 he and Capt. Lyon built a saw-mill on the South Branch, on the lower end of his farm, and engaged in lumbering. He subsequently bought out Mr. Lyon and continued lumbering and farming on a large scale for many years, giving employment to a number of men. In about 1844 he erected a distillery upon his farm, which after two or three years he sold to James Paine and his brother Jeremiah, who removed it to the place of the latter at South Branch. Mr. Blackman was a man well known in the county. Beginning life without a dollar, through careful management, industry and the favor of good luck, he acquired a fine fortune, which he left to his children. He was a liberal supporter of the churches and schools, and the poor man was never turned away from his door. His life, which was a successful one, was closed Dec. 28, 1864.

July 4, 1826, he was joined in marriage with Miss Lovice Rockwood, who was also born at Peru, Mass. She died upon the homestead, Aug. 23, 1883, aged 81 years, 9 mos.

Their children were—

Lyman, born Dec. 4, 1828; married Jane Quackenbaughs, subsequently Mrs. Elizabeth Fox; resides with his brother upon the homestead ;

Daniel R., born June 16, 1830; married Brunette Kellogg, subsequently Mrs. Jemima Hopkins; resides in Monroe;

Judson S., born March 29, 1847; married Cassie Wolf; occupies the ancestral estate.

Libeus Marcy, a native of Connecticut, born June 19, 1793, migrated to Monroe, Bradford county, in 1822, having been induced hither by a brother-in-law, Chester Mason, who came the year before. After residing upon the " Parks place " for a year or two, he traded his property for timber-land, now included in the farms of his son, Lyman, Mrs. Heisz and Mr. Wickham, and in company with Mr. Mason put up a saw-mill and engaged in lumbering for a number of years. After that business ceased to be a great industry, he gave the balance of his life to the improvement of his farm. He was a man of indomitable energy, and fought most successfully the battle of life. Three times he strided the distance between Monroeton and Connecticut on foot, before the present day facilities of travel were known, and when economy and frugality were a necessary part of the common practice of successful life. He was one of Monroe's best citizens, and filled his place well in all the common duties of a citizen; and in promptness met the responsibilities that were conferred upon him by his fellow men. Of littleness and dishonesty he was never accused, and of bad faith he was never suspected. In his advanced age Mr. Marcy enjoyed the fruits of his earlier sacrifices, in the convenience and comforts that gathered around him, and in the beauty and improvement that spread out before him. He died Feb. 28, 1877, on the farm where he lived, reared his family and prospered.

He was twice married, his first wife being Lucy Keeler, who bore him—*Charles*, Aug. 29, 1825, who resides in Monroe.

In 1828 he married Mary Edsall. The children resulting from this marriage were—

Lyman, born April 2, 1829, who occupies the homestead;

Moses M., born Dec. 25, 1831, residing in Terry township;

Eliza J., born Nov. 23, 1832; married Lewis Botree;

Hiram, born June 12, 1835; died in his country's service, Aug. 5, 1863;

Solon, born April 11, 1837; residing in Monroe;

Vinson, born Aug. 31, 1843; residing in Monroe.

Mary Edsall Marcy was born Feb. 6, 1799; died Nov. 2, 1875.

Thomas Lewis, or "Uncle Tommy Lewis," as he was generally known, a native of Lebanon county, Pa., came to Monroe in 1822 from McKunesville, Pa. His first stopping-place was at Fowlertown, where he remained for ten years. He then moved to South Branch on the place now occupied by his son, James H., where he remained until the time of his demise, Jan. 27, 1854, at the age of 74 years.

In 1822 Mr. Lewis was assessed as a "wheelwright," but his business was more nearly that of a cabinet-maker. For years he supplied the people for miles with spinning-wheels (both little and big), chairs, and bedsteads; and articles of his manufacture are in use to this day. He worked faithfully at his trade, till old age required him to quit it. His son, Robert, had purchased a tract of timberland, who with his brother, James, erected a mill on the very site of Harris' mill in 1835, and began the manufacture of lumber James subsequently succeeded to the whole estate and engaged quite extensively in lumbering, till within a few years since his time has been more fully devoted to farming. Thomas Lewis was a man respected for his honesty, and deep religious faith. He was a member of the Presbyterian church for many years. In the rearing of his family he took a great pride, and never did foul or wicked words from his lips blight the characters of his children. He wedded Miss Charlotte Hughes, who bore him—

Mary, who married Jos. Brown and resides at Greenwood;

Robert, who lived and died in Albany;

Charlotte, who died when a young lady;

Margaret, who married James Dewitt, of West Burlington;

James H., who occupies the old farm;

Joseph, who resides at Dushore, Pa.;

Moses M., who occupied a part of the homestead when he died.

Mrs. Lewis died Nov. 27, 1850, aged 72 years, 4 months, 29 days.

Dr. Benoni Mandeville, a native of Granby, Mass., came to Bradford county in 1813, at first settling in Orwell township, where he practiced his profession, and preached for a time. In 1822 he came to Monroe and purchased what is now the W. W. Decker property. He resided in the town and practiced medicine for some thirty years, then removed to Poughkeepsie, N. Y. He was the father of Mrs. S. W. Alden and Rev. Sumner Mandeville, D. D.

Burr Ridgeway, one of the most eminent and interesting characters of the early days of old Bradford, was the son of Daniel and Jane Burr Ridgeway. He was of Quaker descent, and was born in the town of Springfield, Burlington county, N. J., April 17, 1780. When he was eleven years old his father removed to Philadelphia, and was accidentally killed soon thereafter, leaving young Burr at that tender age, without a father's care to shape his future destiny in life's untrodden path. In 1803 he came to Wysox to take charge of John Hollenback's store and house of entertainment. In the following year (1804) he was appointed postmaster for Wysox, which was then the only post-office between Wyalusing and Sheshequin. In the same year (Oct. 10) he was united in marriage with Alice Mozer, widow of the late Nathaniel Mozer, and daughter of Moses and Hannah Shoemaker Coolbaugh, of Wysox. He purchased what is known as the " Piollet farm," but sold it in 1808 and purchased on Wysox creek, where he, in company with one of his brothers, built a saw and grist mill* in 1809 or '10 Not meeting with the success which he had anticipated, and having had ill luck in making his first shipment, he was compelled to abandon the enterprise, and returned to Philadelphia for a year or two. Having earned a little capital he again returned to the county, and in the fall of 1812 went to Towanda to clerk for Wm. Means, of which he speaks thus: " When

---

*This mill occupied the site of where Barns' mill, Rome, now is.

the election came that brought Bradford county into existence, I had resided in the district (partly in Wysox and partly in Orwell, now Rome), and that fall Wm. Means, Esq.,
had brought in a large stock of goods, and agreed with me
to assist him until his eldest son, who was to 'tend the bar
of the tavern and assist me when hurried in the sto re, should
become fully acquainted with the business.

"We did a good fall business. Our new village had no
particular name, and Esq. Means was desirous that it should
be called Meansville ; and as I wanted a lot to build on, he
gave me to understand that if I would assist him, and do all
in my power, he would give me one. Accordingly I chose
a lot (that on which Patton's block now stands), and he asked
me to measure it off and stake it out. He let me have a
small building, formerly occupied as a blacksmith shop, for
a justice's office. In due time I fenced the lot, put up a
house and stable, and also printing office, and lived upon it.
In the meantime, all the letters I wrote, and all the papers I
could get the name of Meansville on, I was careful to do so.
Time passed on and there being no post-office in the place,
a few friends joined together and petitioned the Postmaster
General for one. The petition was heard, and Esq. Means
appointed postmaster. Things went on smoothly, yet there
was no mail route or communication with the Wysox office.
Everyone had to bring and carry his own letters. At length
Mr. Simpson came in with a printing press, and we wanted
a regular mail but could not effect our purpose, and were in
consequence greatly inconvenienced. This was the first year.

"In 1813 I was elected County Commissioner by a majority of 108 votes. Again we represented to the Postmaster General our situation, who gave me the job of carrying the mail to Wysox and back, weekly. I would send my two boys with a pillow case, and get, perhaps, a peck or more of letters and papers. There was not a mail route in the county, except up and down the river, on the east side, once a week.

"After I had purchased the press, Esq. Means was very friendly to me and assisted me in many ways. I was still improving the lot and again asked him for a deed. His reply was, that he had not yet got his patent and did not like to give a deed. I was owing him and offered to give him a judgment, which he was willing to accept, but still refused the deed. Thus things continued until I sold my press, rented my buildings and moved to Wysox, leaving the property in the hands of Esq. Means. Soon after, Gov. Hiester was elected, my friends petitioned him, asking that I be appointed Prothonotary. I received the appointment and soon after entering upon the duties of my office, the State of Pennsylvania commenced the publication of a new map of the State. It was known that I had been many times through the county as Commissioner, and that part of the map pertaining to Bradford county was cut out and sent to me to make any corrections that might be necessary. I observed two or three errors in roads and creeks, and corrected them. Our village on the map was called *Towanda*, which I crossed off, and after substituting Meansville, returned the map. Soon after I read another copy to see if they had made the proper corrections with Meansville on the map in place of

Towanda. I showed it to Esq. Means and now thought my title good, but he seeing that he had gained his point, very bluntly told me that he would give me no deed. Disappointed with his treatment, I erased the name Meansville and again substituted Towanda. At the same time a sensible Legislature, on petition of the citizens of the village, in erecting it into a orough gave it the name of Towarda, and the map was altered to suit. Thus the name of Means passed into the tomb of the Capulets, and I was wronged out of what was worth $500 to me."

Upon the establishment of the post-office at Meansville, Mr. Ridgeway was made deputy postmaster by Mr. Means. On the 15th day of March, 1813, he was appointed a Justice of the Peace by Simon Snyder, for the district comprising the townships of Towanda, Burlington and Wysox.* He was appointed by Chas. F. Welles, deputy Prothonotary, and Register and Recorder, Feb. 17, 1813. In the general election of the same year he was elected County Commissioner. On account of the difficulties attending the publication and distribution of his paper, Thomas Simpson sold the *Bradford Gazette* and press to Mr. Ridgeway, who commenced its publication with the second year (1814). At this time, it should be remembered that there was not a mail route on the west side of the river in the county, and but one on the east side, from Athens to Wilkes-Barre, once a week and back again. When Mr. Ridgeway began publishing the *Gazette* there had been no improvement in mail facilities, but the people were very obliging, and one seemed to vie with

*Chas. F. Welles administered the oath of office to him on the 15th of April.

another in distributing the papers. Petitions were forwarded to the Postmaster General to have a certain mail route established, whereupon he issued proposals for two routes which were to pass through several of the townships of the county for two years, and the mail to be carried on horseback. Mr. Ridgeway became the contractor upon both lines. He continued the publication of the *Gazette* for over three years, when a difficulty arose between C. F. Welles and Samuel McKean, which ended in a lawsuit that was very injurious to the *Gazette*. He therefore sold the press and material to Samuel Streeter and Edwin Benjamin, and turned his attention to agriculture, moving to Wysox, where he had an interest in lands. Upon the election of Joseph Hiester he was appointed Prothonotary and Register and Recorder of the county. His commission was dated Feb. 8, 1821 At the close of Hiester's administration he again turned his attention to farming and went to reside (1822) on an improved tract of land on the South Branch of the Towanda creek. Of his purchase he says: " John D. Sanders, a coarse, rough, hard working, hard drinking, hard swearing man from Maryland, settled without title on a tract of land belonging to the Holland Land Company, on the South Branch of Towanda creek, now included in the farms of Freeman Sweet and others. He made a considerable of a clearing on the tract, and another on the place, now owned by Mr. Blackman. On the latter place he built a saw-mill and stocked it with logs, cut a good many boards, and was prospering finely. He felt so much so, that he said he did not thank Jesus Christ for a living ; but alas ! in the spring,

' the rains descended, and the floods came " and swept away his mill entirely, and most of his lumber. Being an energetic man, he gathered up what boards he could and took them down the river, carrying with him a good supply of counterfeit money. On his return he seemed to have plenty of money, but hearing that a certain man from down the river wanted to see him, he became very uneasy, and offered his farm for sale to many persons, among the number, myself. He wished to sell farming utensils, cattle, &c. I concluded to purchase, both his real and personal property, and having agreed upon terms, we chose W. Keeler, appraiser, and I took the stock, hay, &c., at his appraisement. I paid him all but about $200, and gave my note, with time for the balance." After having resided upon the farm now known as the " Ridgeway place," long enough to get his children started, he returned to Towanda, and continued to act as Justice of the Peace for some years, and for a short time engaged in the mercantile business. After a few years upon the farm again, in 1846 he went to reside in Franklin township. In 1851 he was elected to the office of Town Clerk, and held the same office for the next seventeen years succeeding. And again in 1854, was chosen Justice of the Peace. It is thus seen that there has hardly been another man in the county, who filled so many offices of honor and trust as he ; and that his capacity and integrity were appreciated by his fellow citizens. In 1838 he united with the M. E. church at Monroeton, while under the pastoral charge of Philo E. Brown, and was one of the first trustees after the establishment of the church at the place above named, and was clerk until the time of his removal to Franklin. He ardently espoused and enjoyed the comforting influences and blessings of his religious faith ; and up to the last he bore his privations and afflictions with Christian fortitude and uncomplaining patience. In 1868 he was deprived of his eyesight, but retained full control of his mental faculties till the very last, almost reaching the age of a centenarian. He was a member (one of the first in the county) of the Masonic order, and though his death was not generally known, his funeral cortege was nearly a mile long. He was an esteemed citizen, and one of the most popular and useful citizens the county ever had.

Mr. Ridgeway's death occurred Aug. 19, 1876, and his remains are interred beside those of his companion, at Franklindale.

The children of Burr and Alice Ridgeway were—

Hannah M., born July 22, 1805; married Geo. Tracy; resides at Monroeton, and is still a very bright and entertaining lady;

David, born Nov. 1, 1806; succeeded to the ancestral estate, which is now occupied by his widow and sons; died Sept. 2, 1864;

James C., born Aug. 28, 1808; resided upon a farm in Franklin; died Sept. 21, 1878;

Lydia A., born July 6, 1810; married Thomas T. Simley; resides at Monroeton;

Mary E., born July 26, 1814; married Joseph Johnson; died Feb 15, 1857;

Nancy J., born April 25, 1816; married Freeman Sweet, of Monroe; died July 6, 1875.

Mrs. Ridgeway was born Feb. 7, 1780; died June 8, 1858. For many years she was a member of the church of Christ and adorned her Christian profession by a suitable walk and conversation, and by her meekness and gentleness of disposition secured the respect and esteem of many friends —while she was exemplary in the midst of her family, an intelligent and provident wife, and a wise and kind mother. The remembrance of her amiable character will long be deeply cherished.

The Masons.—The history of this family can be traced back to the time of Cromwell, in whose army, one of the Masons served as a drummer, and was killed in battle. He left three sons, John, Robert and Nathaniel, who emigrated to America. *John* settled in Hartford, Conn., and is no other than the interesting "Captain John Mason" of Pequod renown

Robert, the ancestor of the Masons of Bradford county, settled in Boston. A grandson, Robert, settled at Ashford, Conn., where he purchased land at a penny an acre. He was the great-grandfather of the three Masons, who settled in Monroe.

Eliphalet Mason, the son of Deacon Ebenezer and Mary Hastings Mason, was born in the town of Ashford, Windham county, Conn., June 23, 1780.

At the age of fourteen years he went to Springfield, Mass., to learn the trade of a shoemaker with an uncle; but it not proving congenial to his tastes, he returned to his

father's farm after a year. Here for the next two years succeeding his time was spent diligently in tilling the soil, and
assisting in his father's cooper-shop, during stormy days.

Having been converted to God (at seventeen years) and
joined the Congregational church, on account of feeble
health, he concluded to prepare for the ministry. But his
education was too limited, and he appealed to his father for
aid. With a large family to provide for, the father could
give him no other encouragement than to offer him his time,
with the privilege of getting all the knowledge he desired,
but must pay for it himself. The offer was accepted, and he
began his studies under the Rev. Enoch Pond, doing chores
nights and mornings for his grandmother for his board. His
instructor proved an excellent one and he progressed finely.
Among other things, he was required to write compositions,
and was much praised in making verse. In addition to his
regular studies, he was given lesssons in voice culture, which,
though he had natural musical talents), proved a great comfort and benefit to him in early life. Just when the aspiring,
ambitious student began to think that his fond hopes should
soon be realized, Fate turned against him.

His grandmother died, and soon after the wife of Rev.
Mr. Pond, which left him without a boarding place, and so
affected his tutor that he did not recite for weeks. Finally
he abandoned the idea of a college education. While prose-
cuting his studies under the Rev. Mr. Pond, Mr. Perley Coburn was also a student. A strong attachment grew up between the two young men, and from 1799 to 1801, Mr.
Mason was a frequent visitor at the house of Mr. Coburn's

father. In fact, the charming Zilpah had very much at-
tracted his attentions, and became his first love. At this
juncture the young lady's father moved with the family to
Pennsylvania, whither the smitten Eliphalet had secretly resolved to go also, as soon as he had earned sufficient means.
For more than a year he worked at coopering at Hartford,
Simsburry and Wintonburry, in the meantime giving attention to the composition of music, which resulted in the pro-
duction of a song-book, entitled *The Complete Pocket Song-
Book*, which became quite popular.

In May, 1802, he started for Pennsylvania on horse-back
to find the object of his early affections. After a journey of
six days he reached Nanticook, and leaving his horse there,
footed his way through the wilderness, a distance of ten
miles, to Mr. Coburn's settlement (then Orwell.) On the
22d of June (1802) he and Zilpah were married. During
his stay in the West he erected an old-fashioned spring
pole foot lathe by using old chain links for gudgeons, and
with a sap-tree gouge and framing chisel for his tools,
manufactured six kitchen chairs and two spinning wheels,
the first known in that part of the county. After two weeks
he returned to Connecticut. In October, 1802, he bid fare-
well to the State of his nativity, and again set out for Pennsylvania, reaching Orwell (now Warren) in the early part of
November. He says: " My all as regards property was a
horse, saddle and bridle, portmanteau and thirty-one cents
in money. The horse I soon afterwards sold for $60."
During the first winter of his residence in the county he
taught a school of three months in Wysox, and instructed

in music at Towanda, Wysox, and at the mouth of Sugar Creek. His patrons at Wysox having been so well pleased with his teaching hired him to continued the school for a year. In the midst of his prosperity Zilpah was attacked with fever, and died in a few days (June 15, 1803.) He says: "Every place wore a gloom to me; I was among strangers, and all my youthful hopes were gone. I now determined to to leave this wilderness land," and try my fortune in some older country. Money was very scarce, and I had to take my pay for teaching in wheat. Finally by reducing my bills half, I succeeded in getting a few dollars of the more wealthy families. Steering for the "Sunny South," I crossed the ferry at Towanda. I told Wm. Means, Esq., my plans, who finally discouraged me, and induced me to remain and teach the school in his district for the winter. His children had attended my school at Wysox, being required to cross the river on a boat, and walk two miles. I taught my school of four months at Towanda, and also during the winter a singing school, in an adjoining district at the forks of the Towanda Creek (Monroeton.) Spring came and I was still determined to continue my journey. Reed Brockaway, Esq., prevailed upon my teaching a school in his district during the summer (1804), which I finally consented to. I was pleased with the people in this section, especially the younger class, and became intimately acquainted with Miss Roxy, the daughter of Gordon Fowler, whom, in the course of time, I concluded to marry. In anticipitation of this event, I purchased of Reed Brockaway, Esq., his property, consisting of twelve acres of improved land, with a log-house thereon, located where the village of Monroeton now is. Here I concluded to make my future home. * * * In the latter part of the summer I attended court, as a witness at Wilkes-Barre, then "the county seat of Luzerne, (which included Bradford, not yet formed." On the 22d of October, 1804, Mr. Mason and Roxy Fowler were married. During the winter of 1804-5 he worked at coopering in Lancaster county, Pa., returning to Monroe again in March. That spring, in company with Abner C. Rockwell, they made up a raft of lumber and took it down the river. After returning from this trip he went to Northumberland county, Pa., and engaged in teaching school until September; when he says: " After tarrying home for about two weeks, in company with Rogers Fowler, Russell Fowler, Abner C. Rockwell, Daniel Miller and Warner Ladd, we went to explore the county, through the wilderness in a direct line to Northumberland. We went up the south branch of the Towanda Creek, leaving it at the Old French saw-mill, which was the last trace of settlement on this side of the mountain."

Upon reaching Northumberland all the party, save Mr. Mason, started back, he remaining in the county during the winter teaching, singing and day school. In the fall of 1806 Mr. Mason says: " In company with my father-in-law and brother-in-law, Jonathan Fowler, we manufactured 250 barrels, and floated them down the river to Wilkes-Barre, and sold them, but did not much more than realize expenses." In the winter of 1806-7 he taught again at Monroeton, and in the spring of 1807 at Towanda, continuing for six months. On the 24th day of October, 1807, he was

commissioned a Justice of the Peace by Gov. Thomas Mc-
Kean, for the county of Luzerne, and held that office continually till it was made elective by the State Constitution.
He now began giving some attention to farming, and in the
spring of 1808 sold his framed home at Fowlertown (erected
fall of 1806) to Russell Fowler, and purchased a possession
of 120 acres on the Towanda road, a mile from Monroeton.
Here he erected a house and moved in with his family in
October. During the summer of 1809 he was engaged in
digging a mill-race for Wm. Means on the Towanda Creek,
at what is now known as the White place. In the fall of the
same year he entered into partnership with Lorenzo Harvy,
for the purpose of erecting a saw mill, on the creek, where
Masontown now is. After having built a house and made
some progress upon the mill, Mr Harvey sold out his interest to Dr. Asa C. Whitney, the new firm, at once, proced-
ing to the completion of the mill. In 1810 Mr. Mason sold
his share also, and Whitney became the sole owner.

In October (1810) he was one of the judges of the general
election for Towanda and carried the returns to Wilkes-
Barre, thence to Bethlehem with the vote for Congress. In
the fall of 1811, Mr. Mason says : " I had concluded to com-
mence the mercantile business, there being no store kept on
the Towanda side of the river. Wm. Means, Esq., having
suspended business, at least for a short time, left the country without goods for the consumption of the settlers." He
continued in this business for two years, then being unable
to collect his bills, and his creditors taking advantage of his
embarrassment, he was compelled to abandon the enter-

prise. In 1812 he erected the first steam distillery ever known in Bradford county. Mr. Mason says : " In the winter of 1813–14 I taught a school in the school-house standing where the village of Monroeton now is. During my teaching Wm. Weston, with his brother, John, then a young man of about twenty years, came to the place to instruct in the art of writing. They taught in my school and I took lessons of them. In the spring of 1814 I entered into an agreement with the young man, John, since Doctor Weston, to take a tour with him in the southern part of the State to instruct in this art. On the first of September I returned without having earned more than enough to pay expenses." In the fall of 1814 Mr. Mason was commissioned Lieutenant of militia, and with others was drafted in the war of 1812. A company of 110 men was raised and placed under his command and sent to Danville, awaiting orders ; but returned home after a month's absence. At the October election (1814) he was elected Auditor of Bradford county for the term of three years, being the only Democrat elected on the ticket. From April, 1815, he acted as deputy Sheriff, under A. C. Rockwell, till the close of his term, and transacted nearly all the business connected with the office. In 1816 Mr. Mason moved to Towanda with his family, being the twelfth within what is now the borough limits. In the summer of that year, in company with Jonathan Fowler he erected a saw-mill " on the falls of a small stream flowing into the South Branch at the head of Fowler's mill-pond," on a plat of land belonging to the Asylum Land Company, which he contracted for. · Again in the fall of 1816 he was honored with office, being elected County Commissioner over his brother-in-law, A. C. Rockwell, the Federal candidate. Mr. Mason says : " In the spring of 1817 grain was very scarce Corn had been ruined by the frosts of the fall before, and every kind of food was scarce. It became evident that some one must undertake to supply the village with meat, and as I could best afford the time the task fell upon me. Indeed, so great was the dependence on me that the villagers could not boil the pot without my providing."

In the summer of 1818, I burned a kiln of brick, which I mostly struck or moulded with my own hands, having become somewhat acquainted with that kind of business while living in Hartford." July 1, 1818, he was commissioned by Gov. Findlay, Recorder of Deeds, &c. and in conjunction with the Prothonotary to administer oaths to such persons as might be appointed by the Governor. In the same month he was also directed by the Governor to administer the oath of office to the Hon. Edward Herrick, who had been appointed President Judge of the 13th Judicial District, composed of the counties of Bradford, Susquehanna and Tioga. For something like a year he was then engaged in selling groceries at Towanda. Having purchased of Gurdon Hewitt, the mill which he erected in 1809, he again moved with his family to Monroe in April, 1821. During that year he built a half mile of the Susquehanna and Tioga turnpike, through the wilderness between Towanda and Sugar Creek. In 1824, he was appointed a commissioner with Edward Eldred and William Brindle to lay out a State Road from Muncy to Towanda. While thus employed, he also received the appointment of Deputy Surveyor for Bradford county. Again in 1829, he was elected to the office of County Commissioner, having a greater majority than his opponent had votes. In 1830 he was appointed agent for the Asylum Company's lands, and in 1834 was directed to take charge of large tracts of lands belonging to Clement S. Miller, of Philadelphia, who sent out a Mr. Jones, a practical geologist to search for minerals. About a month after Mr. Mason and Jones, began their explorations, they discovered that the highlands of Mr. Miller in Bradford county contained valuable beds of bituminous coal and by sinking shafts in many places found that it extended over the most of his land on the north side of the Schrader branch. In 1837, Mr. Mason and his son, Gordon F., became the purchaser of several thousand acres of land, lying in Bradford county, which the Asylum Company had been anxious to dispose of. The investment was a good one, and the purchasers realized a handsome little fortune. Mr. Mason continued in active and varied business till 1844, when he started his children in the world, and threw off most of his cares to enjoy his closing days. He found great comfort in making verse, reading his papers, and frequently contributing an article to the press. His writings will be remembered by many under the *sobriquet* of "Old South." In his younger days he had given considerable attention to the sciences ; thus becoming a diligent student of nature, his poetry was sound and logical. Mr. Mason was a man of genius, indomitable energy, and undaunted courage. His honesty and integrity were never questioned, and of littleness he was never accused. His life was a successful one, and a noble example. In the rearing of his family he took a great pride, and gave each of his children a good start in life. In 1802 Mr. Mason joined the Masonic order and remained a member, until old age compelled him to withdraw. For several years prior to his death, his eyes gave him much pain, being at times a great privation ; but he was blessed with a most remarkable degree of mental vigor, till death silenced his tongue forever. His demise occurred March 11, 1853.

The children of Eliphalet and Roxy Mason were—

Zilpha, born Jan. 26, 1806; married Isaac Rogers, of Monroe ;

Roxy, born Dec. 10 1807; married Charles Birch, of Monroe ;

Gordon F., born Jan. 19, 1810; married Mary A. Mason ; resided in Towanda ; dealt extensively in real estate, etc. ;

Rufus, born Jan. 31, 1812; married Elizabeth Foster, of Towanda ;

E. Hastings, born April 28, 1815; married Phylindia Woodruff, of Monroe; studied medicine and practiced at Towanda ;

William A., born Sept. 29, 1819; married Mary A. Cheeney, of Windham ; resides at Laporte ; civil engineer, and ex-side Judge of Sullivan Co. ;

Lemuel A., born March 22, 1821; died when a young man ;

Sarah, born Feb. 4, 1826; married Jacob Veiley, of Troy.

Roxy Fowler Mason, born July 16, 1786; died Feb. 15, 1851.

Ebenezer Mason, born Oct. 2, 1782, came to Monroe through the influence of his brother, Eliphalet, in the fall of 1820. During Adams' administration, in apprehension of war with France, upon the organization of the militia companies, Mr. Mason enlisted but was never called out, conciliatory measures having been adopted. In 1821, he returned to Connecticut and brought in his family, being also accompanied by his brother Chester, who now also came to live in the West. Ebenezer came in to work at his trades. He was a cooper, carpenter, wagon-maker, and gunsmith. In fact it is said " that he could mend or make anything that was possible." He put up a shop in connection with his brother's saw mill, and met the people's wants in the mechanical line. After some years he purchased the place now occupied by his son, Wm. J., and alternated his trades with farming. He was an industrious, hard-working man. His demise occurred May 10, 1873.

His wife, Martha Harwood, bore him—

Mehitable, who married Moses Kellogg;

Henrietta, born June 10, 1806; married John Needham and moved west;

William J., born May 4, 1809; married Sarah Lantz, of Franklin, and resides upon the homestead;

Rufus, born Oct. 1, 1810; went to Ohio, when a young man; studied medicine and is still a practitioner,

Mary A., born Feb. 26, 1813; married G. F. Mason, of Towanda;

Martha, born April 29, 1815 ; married D. F. Miller ;

Margaret, born Feb. 15, 1817 ; married Daniel F. Miller, of Albany ;

Margaret, born Nov. 16, 1819 ; married Charles Boyles ;

David, born May 2, 1822 ; married Mary Steel ;

Harriet, born Dec. 24, 1824 ; married Anthony Mullen ;

Alonzo, born Aug. 13. 1813 ; married Elizabeth Simpson.

Martha Harwood Mason was born Nov. 28, 1780; died Feb. 27, 1868.

Chester Mason, born June 10, 1793, as already stated, came to Monroe in 1821. He was a cooper by trade but gave attention to lumbering and farming. He occupied the Park's place, and died there. He was an honest, sober, industrious, thorough-going Yankee. His death occurred Nov. 25, 1843.

His wife, Clarissa Marcy, bore him—

Amelia, who married Samuel R. Mason, of Philadelphia; *Laura*, who married Isaac Foster, of Monroe ; *John*, who married Elizabeth Ingham, and resides in Canton ; *Alva*, who went to the gold regions when a young man.

Jeremiah Blackman, born in Connecticut, June 6, 1804, emigrated to the State of New York, when four years of age, with his father's family. In 1825 he joined his brothers in Monroe and worked at his trade—that of blacksmithing, in connection with farming. After a few years he moved three miles farther up the creek to what is known as South Branch, and engaged in farming, blacksmithing, lumbering and hotel keeping.

He was united in marriage with Jane Edsall, who bore

him—*Lucinda* (Mrs. Chester Carter); *William H.*, who moved to Iowa, and died here; *Lamira* (Mrs. Christopher Platt); *Saphronia* (Mrs. Edward Wilcox).

Mr. Blackman's death occurred upon the homestead February 17, 1878; and that of his wife, April 24, 1881, aged 74 years, 7 months and 4 days.

Elizer Sweet, a native of Rhode Island. born July 9, 1778, found his way into Pennsylvania not far from the year 1800. He had become enamored with Miss Amy Wilcox, before her people migrated from the East; hence it is obvious why he was moved to settle in a new country. In the course of time, the Wilcoxes moved into Albany, and Mr. Sweet and Amy became man and wife. It is quite certain that he followed his wife's people into that township, and resided there for a short time, also; then moved to Spencer, N. Y., where he remained till 1819, when he returned to Albany and worked upon the turnpike. In 1826 he moved into Monroe (now (Asylum), and after two or three changes, upon a farm between Monroeton and Liberty Corners. He was a man especially noted for his muscular powers, and is said to have been quite a match for Freeman Wilcox, who was then considered the most powerful man in Northern Pennsylvania. Mr. Sweet's usual weight was about 160 pounds. His death occurred April 1, 1866.

His children were—

Miama, who married Roswell Phillips, and died at Dushore, Pa.;

Rosina, who married Dr. Daniel Cole, of Asylum, and died in Ohio;

Jemima, who married Price Streetor, and died in the West ;

Freeman, born October 19, 1810, married Miss Nancy J., daughter of Burr Ridgeway, and is a highly respected citizen of the township. For a number of years he engaged in lumbering, but has devoted the last part of his life to farming. Beginning in the world, as he expressed it, without a dollar, through industry, economy, and the favor of good luck, earned a handsome fortune and was thus enabled to assist his children in starting in life ; a duty which he proudly performed "Uncle Freeman," as he is commonly called, has always enjoyed the confidence of the people, and has not unfrequently been called to offices of trust, in which he has always demonstrated ability and integrity. Inheriting his father's strength, in his younger days he never met his match in a lift, or in a wrestle. With the kindness of a noble mother's heart, it has always been a pleasure for him to assist his fellow men, and he lives honored and respected by all. Of his family of eight children, but two sons survive, he having also lost his wife July 6, 1875. His elder son, Dallis J., the present Sheriff of Bradford County, was born November 3, 1843, and remained upon his father's farm, until eighteen years of age, when he gave his services to his country and entered the 141st Regiment, P. V., as a private. Although only a boy he rose to the rank of a Sergeant, before the close of the war. In 1868 he engaged in the mercantile business at Monroeton, which he has pursued ever since. In 1870 he was appointed Postmaster, and held the office till Jan., 1885, when he resigned.

In August, 1884, he was nominated by the Republican County Convention as a candidate for Sheriff. His candidacy proved very popular, and he was elected by a vote of 8,426, the greatest ever cast for Sheriff in the county, against 4,096 for his opponent. Mr. Sweet lives in retirement, with his son, *Theron*, upon his farm at South Branch.

Lavina married E. C. Kellogg ;

Hiram married Mary Terwilliger, and resides in Monroe ;

Ransom married Mary Jacoba, and moved to New Jersey, where he died.

Jane married Geo. Irvine, of Monroe ;

Elizabeth married Lyman Hollon, of Monroe ;

Amy, wife of Elizer Sweet, who is remembered as a most endearing lady, was born Aug. 7, 1785 ; died Jan. 8, 1867.

Henry Bassett Myer, born near Ashbury, Sussex county, N. J., September 9, 1805, removed with his father, Jacob Myer and family to Forty Fort, Pa., in 1812; then a year later to Mehoopany, and finally to Bradford county in 1824. After about two years in Franklin township, he purchased a farm in Monroe—the same as now occupied by Clay Rockwell, erected a mill on the place, and engaged in lumbering till 1844, since which time he has given attention to droving, butchering, etc.

In 1840 he was united in marriage with Sarah Gaskill, widow of the late Job Gaskill, of Rochester, N. J., and daughter of Martin and Esther Wallace Young, formerly of Geneva, N. Y. She was a sister of Edward F. Young, the foundry man.

The fruits of this union were—

George V., of Towanda, agent for pensions and patents, and well known to the county as an engineer and ex-county surveyor. He was a gallant soldier and rose to the rank of Captain in Company K, of the 50th Regiment, P. V.

Berlin F., of the firm of Sweet & Co, Monroeton;

Esther, the wife of Eli Griggs, of Grundy, Iowa;

Ella A., the wife of D. J. Sweet;

Charles M., engaged in the butchering business at Towanda.

Ann M., the wife of Will J. Devoe, of Greenwood.

Mr. and Mrs. Myer are yet living together as man and wife, (she born Jan. 12, 1806), and give promise of a much greater longevity. Mr. Myer was one of the original trustees of the Baptist Church at Monroeton.

In 1825 the following were also assessed in Monroe: Adam Beam, Samuel Campbell, Marcus Campbell, Sherman Havens and William Cox; in 1826, William Black, clothier and spinner; in 1827, Joseph Ingham and John Black, both clothiers; in 1828, Orrin Galpin; in 1829, Gashun Harris, Geo. A. McClen; 1830, Clark Cummings, Moses Coolbaugh, Joseph Griggs, Elisha Harris, John E. Ingham (physician); in 1831, Fisher and Wilson, merchants; in 1832, Francis Bull, John Gale, Hanson & Warford, (merchants); in 1833, Thos. T. Smiley; in 1834, Joab Summers, John Campbell (miller), D. M. Bull; in 1835, Nicholas Wanck, Jeremiah Hollon, Elijah Horton; in 1838, James Blauvelt, and Coonrad Mingos.

Joseph Ingham, a native of Yorkshire, England, emigrated to America in 1822. He was a clothier by trade, and was required to smuggle his passage. After a voyage of forty days he landed at Philadelphia, with a sixpence in cash. He worked at his trade for five years in the southern part of the State, then in company with his brother-in-law, John Black, came to Monroe. He rented A. C. Rockwell's factory, and gave attention to carding and dressing cloth. He improved the factory, and manufactured cloth, said to have been the first shop-made in the county. In 1831 he built a factory on the very site of Hawes' toy shops, and did a fine business till 1855, when it was so crippled by the railroad company that he closed his factory. In 1863 he removed to Knoxville, Tioga county, Pa., where he established an extensive business. He was the father of Capt. James B. Ingham, of the 50th P. V., and H. H. Ingham, of Monroeton.

George A. McClen, born at Addison, Vt., May 4, 1810, found his way into Monroe in 1829, and resided in the township, generally, thenceforward until the time of his demise—May 31, 1885. He was the father of S. M. McClen, of Towanda, a member of the Germania band.

Joseph Griggs, a native of Windham, Conn., came to the township in 1830. He located at Monroeton and engaged in farming. He was born Dec. 13, 1783; died Sept. 12, 1874. His children were *Permelia, Mary, John M., Lucius E., Julia A.,* and *Eli.* Mrs. Griggs was born May 26, 1790; died Dec. 14, 1866.

Dr. John Ellicott Ingham, whose father was one of the first settlers in Sugar Run, after having graduated in medicine, located at Monroe in 1830. Four years thereafter he was united in marriage with Miss Amanda, daughter of Judge

Harry Morgan, of Wysox. He built up an extensive practice, and remained in the township for twenty-seven years, then removed to Wysox, where he died in 1857. He was a man of great worth in the community. Soon after coming to Monroe he organized a Union Sabbath-school—the first in the town; and about the same time a temperance society. He also instituted a grammar school for the benefit of young men and women, and instructed them gratuitously. He took a deep interest in his young friends, and in many other ways bestowed his kindness and generosity. His course created a love for study, and had a noble influence in the formation of character. He was endowed with a big heart, and worked to alleviate the pains of his fellow mortals, whether rich or poor. He was a just man, and a noble example. His widow survives him, and resides at Corning, N. Y.

John Gale, a native of Orange county, N. Y., and grandson of Selah Arnout, became a permanent resident of the town in 1832. He was an industrious, hard-working man. His son, Eli, occupies the farm which he cleared up and improved.

Francis Bull located in Monroe in 1835. He was a native of Swarkeston, Derby Co., England, and was born Jan. 21, 1777. He emigrated to America with his brother, John, and reached Philadelphia, Sept. 5, 1801. After remaining at White Hall for a year he came to what is now Elkland, Sullivan county. In 1806 he married Miss Mary E. Lambert, whose father was among the early settlers in Forks township, Sullivan County. Upon making Monroe his home, he settled the farm now occupied by U. M. Pratt, where he died Jan. 22, 1863. Mrs. Bull was also born in the county of Derby, England, September 29, 1789, and died December 26, 1851.

The children of Francis and Mary E. Bull were—*Sarah* (Mrs. J. R. Irvine); *Mary* (Mrs. Luman Pratt); *Francis, Samuel, Joseph, Robert, George, Elizabeth* (Mrs. Daniel Derby), *William, Annie* (Mrs. Thos. G. Dripps), *John*. Of the family only two are now living in the county—Joseph at Liberty Corners, and Robert, known as " 'Squire Bull," in Asylum.

Joah Summers, born in Northumberland, Pa., in 1800, settled at Liberty Corners in 1834. At an early age he was left an orphan, and went to live with his grandfather, Geo. Bird, of Sullivan county. When eleven years of age he had an encounter which, but for a timely rescue, would have cost him his life. He was searching for the cows in the dusk of evening, and hearing some thing behind him he looked around, and was terrified to behold a panther squatted before him. He realized his situation in a twinkling, and though nearly frightened out of his senses, he screamed, Murder! then wheeled and started to run. But as soon as he turned his back to the foe, the panther sprang upon him and crushed him to the ground. He made a feeble struggle, but it availed nothing as he was a mere toy in the clutches of so formidable a beast. The animal fastened its fangs into his cheek, and was soon sucking out his life blood. When almost dead, with a cheek torn away, a hand crushed, and a body dangerously wounded, his cries having been heard, his rescuers arrived, and with some effort beat off the animal and saved his life. His escape was a most miraculous one, and it was thought that he could never get well. However, in the course of time, his wounds healed, and now at the age of eighty-five years he is able to recite his thrilling adventure. We should also state that he has outlived the panther by seventy-four years, and that his life has been a successful and prosperous one. His history is the same old story, full of interest, and noble manhood, that is found in the lives of all self-made men. Having become skilled in the art of weaving, he followed that trade for some years.

In 1831 he was united in marriage with Miss Sally Hollon, of Chemung, N. Y.

The fruits of this union are—

John H., merchant at Monroeton ; and *Angeline E.*, the wife of S. O. Decker, of Liberty Corners.

Mr. Summers is a man greatly esteemed by his neighbors, and has been a life-long consistent and devoted member of the M. E. Church.

Mrs. Summers, born March 29, 1810, is yet living in almost full vigor of her mental and physical powers, and administers most tenderly to the wants of her aged companion.

Jeremiah Hollon, born in Massachusetts, April 6, 1785, was left fatherless, when a small boy, enduring the severe hardships of those days, which made a man of him to be admired in after-years. He was a man of deep religious principles, being among the foremost in establishing means of worshing, many times opening his own house for that purpose.

In 1809 he married Betsy Orcutt, from near Lake Champlain, and settled in Chemung county, N. Y., where
they had a family of fourteen children, four of whom
died. In 1835 Mr. Hollon moved to Monroe and located in
the district, which was named in his honor, and is still known
as Hollon Hill or Liberty Corners. In September, 1851,
his wife died, and he in June, 1871, leaving the following children, all of whom live within a radius of four miles of each
other, and all save Daniel O., of North Towanda, still in the
township of their adoption.

Sally, the wife of Joab Summers; *Charles; Daniel O.;
Deborah*, the wife of Guy C. Irvine; *Eliza*, the wife of Wm.
Irvine; *Lynan G.; Lydia*, the wife of Daniel Cook, de-
ceased; *Almira*, the wife of James W. Irvine; *Harry S.;
William.*

Mr. Hollon married for his second wife Emma Burt, of
Chemung, who survived him a number of years.

Elijah H. Horton moved to Liberty Corners the same year
that Mr. Hollon came in, and cleared up the farm now occupied by J. W. Irvine.

James Blauvelt came to the hill from Chemung county,
N. Y., in 1838, and in 1843 purchased the farm upon which
he now resides.

Coonrad Mingos also settled at Liberty Corners in 1838,
upon the place now occupied by his son, Joseph. He lived
to be nearly 96 years of age and is the oldest person buried
at Liberty Corners.

George Gilpin, not far from 1832, moved up Kent Run to

the place now occupied by Clark Johnson, being the first settler there.

William North, a native of Yorkshire, E:gland, born in 1775, emigrated to America in 1820. For a time he resided in Northumberland county, Pa., where he married Mrs. Jane Smith *nee* Jane Fisher. He was a clothier by trade, and in 1832 came to Monroe and rented Mr. Fowler's factory, which he subsequently purchased. He improved the facilities and did a flattering business. He died Dec. 21, 1868, and his son, Benjamin, succeeds him in the same business. *Mary* (Mrs. Gould Phinney) is a daughter, and *William,* a second son, resides in Philadelphia.

Larry Dunmore, Nathan Brown, Thomas Smith and *John Edsall* were among the early settlers up the South Branch. Smith settled the Blackman place ; Brown the place afterwards occupied by his son, Henry ; and Edsall the place afterwards occupied by his son, George. —— McIntyre, Wm. Cox and Mr. Dunmore had occupied the Edsall place, respectively.

Charles Brown was born in Wysox, Oct. 16, 1808. In 1837 he purchased a mill property at Greenwood and for several years engaged in lumbering. Quitting that business he devoted his time to farming, and continued until the time of his demise, Jan. 28, 1874. Mr. Brown was known as the " horse farrier, and was called for miles to pronounce diseases. His knowledge of the horse was wonderful, and he seemed to determine his disease almost intuitively. His widow, " Delight Wilcox," resides upon the homestead.

George Tracy, a son of Solomon Tracy, one of the early

settlers of Ulster, engaged in the mercantile business at Towanda for about two years, then in 1832 moved to Monroeton, where he continued the same business in connection with
lumbering. The last years of his life he devoted to farming.
He served one term as Associate Judge of Bradford county,
held the office of Justice of the Peace, etc. He was the father
of *Dr. Geo. P.* Tracy, of Burlington; *Burr R.* Tracy, of
Washington, D. C., now engaged in the real estate business,
and *Henry C.* Tracy, for many years a merchant at Monroeton.

Squatters at an early day made beginnings in different parts
of the township, but moved away after a short time. On the
Summers place a log distillery and log house had been erected and covered with clapboards. In 1813 the clearings were
covered with a second growth of timbers, fully four inches in
thickness. This was known as the " Butler Clearing," the
one on the Coolbaugh place as " Parker Meadows," and that
on the Salisbury place as the " Massaker Clearing." These
improvements are supposed to have been made by people
who came in under the Connecticut title, but left after they
had been despoiled of their possessions.

HABITS AND CUSTOMS.

Money, the pioneers had none; and they were required to
dress in the plainest and least expensive manner. Their common *habiliments* were pantaloons and dresses, made from flax
for summer wear, and from wool for winter. " Buckskin
trousers " were in fashion, and were not unfrequently worn by
the men and boys. A. L. Cranmer, Esq., counted the weal-

thiest man in Monroe, wore such when a boy. Roundabouts, or sailors' jackets, took the place of coats.

Calico was less common than silk is now, and cost seventy-five cents per yard. She that could afford a dress made from seven yards of this material, wore " an extravagant garment." " The fashion was petticoats and short gowns." Shawls were made from pressed woolen cloth, and the finest home-made linen was bleached, and constructed into fine shirts for men and boys.

A lady's common dress was " copperas and white," as it was called, and " copperas and blue, two and two " for nice.

The women wore handkerchiefs, as a covering for the head, or bonnets of their own manufacture. It was not a strange occurrence to see a young lady, with her shoes and stockings in her hand, and a handkerchief about her head, while on her way to " meeting," in the log school house, or at some neighbor's cabin. When upon nearing the place of worship, she would sit down by the road-side and dress her feet. Garments were made to wear the longest possible, as it was very uncertain when the next could be had.

The boys had hats and caps, made by their mothers, from woolen cloth or straw, and sometimes, perhaps, from raccoon skins. Some wore knit caps, also, until " seal-skin caps," as they were called, came in fashion.

Garments were fastened together with buttons constructed out of thread.

Nearly every wife had her spinning-wheel and loom, and manufactured her own cloth. Each did her own coloring, and the bark from a soft maple tree, hemlock, butternut or

" witch hazel " was used for dying purposes, also log-wood and smart-weed. Copperas, alum, and sorrel were used to set the colors.

During the summer season the boys, girls and women, generally, went barefooted, as did some of the men. Rattle-snakes were without number, and were a great dread to the boys, when in search of the cows.

In the winter shoes with leggins were worn. Frequently it happened that some of the poorer families had no shoes, in which case the boys would heat large chips, to stand upon to keep their feet warm while chopping wood.

But few of the men had a "dress-up" suit. This consisted of *knee-breeches*, ornamented with buckles, long stockings, made from cotton, wool or silk, and shoes with buckles.

Samuel Cranmer, the Fowlers and a few others wore a " dress-up."

A lady's "dress-up" generally consisted of a linsey-woolsey suit, improved by pressing.

The food of the pioneers was coarse, and consisted of corn and rye bread, sometimes wheat, with potatoes. The last were generally baked in the fire-place, by covering them with, ashes and coals. Mush and milk was not an uncommon diet. Venison could be had in abundance, for the killing, and brook trout for the catching. Deer and bear meat was made more appetizing by smoking it. Jerked venison was also a favorite article on the bill of fare. Sometimes bread was made out of wheat and rye bran. Milk was the main dependence, and was made a most palatable dish in several ways.

Stoves were not in use, and baking was done in fire-places

and stove bake ovens. The raw material for bread and cake was prepared and put in the bake-kettle (a low kettle-shaped iron pot with a cover), which was then placed over coals on the hearth-stone. Upon the cover of the kettle coals were also placed that the baking would be more evenly done. " Johnny cakes " were baked in the long-handled frying-pans, which were heated over the fire-places. The bake-kettle remained in use for some years, when it was supplanted by the tin oven.

Maple sugar was used for sweetening purposes, and corn-cobs were burned in the bake kettle cover to get a substitute for saleratus. Maple syrup and honey took the place of butter, and bear's fat was used for shortening. Fried cakes were baked in pots of bear and raccoon fat. There not being many maple groves in Monroe, the pioneers frequently went to some neighboring settlement in the spring, and made sugar and syrup.

Browned rye, peas, beech-nuts, chestnuts and chickery were substituted for coffee, and sage, thyme, peppermint, spearmint, evans root, spice bush, sweet fern, pansy and hemlock boughs for tea. Imported tea and coffee were too costly, and could only be afforded when the " good mothers " had company. Moreover it could not be had, Jacob Bowman and Wm. Means brought in an occasional load of goods, but limited each family to a pound of coffee, and a half pound of tea, which lasted for a year. One lady says: " Jacob Bow-man made a trip to the city, and, among other things, brought in some gingham, which we paid six shillings a yard for."

Herbs of all kinds were gathered and used for teas in sickness, and each had its specific cure. For instance, elderblow, cat-nip and worm-wood were used for children, and bone-set, pennyroyal, etc., for adults.

Greased Paper, hung over an opening in the wall, afforded light for the cabins in the day-time. At night they were illuminated by the light, given out from the huge fire-places, and pick pine splinters stuck into the chimney jambs. This furnished sufficient light for the mothers to sew, spin and weave by ; for the fathers to mend and make shoes, and the boys and girls to get their lessons.

"Aunt Mary Bull" says: "Many a time I have sewed till eleven o'clock at night by the light of a pitch-pine knot."

A supply of pitch-pine knots was generally put in before winter. Deer fat and lard were sometimes used for illuminating purposes, but not frequently.

Tallow lamps were finally introduced, and were used when tallow could be had, or lard spared. They were a cup-like construction, to contain animal fats, and could be hung against the wall. One end of a piece of cloth, answering as a wick, was dropped into the cup and the other end, which hung out, was lighted.

Tallow candles next followed, and subsequently lamps for burning coal oil.

—The time of day was determined by "sun marks" or noon marks, upon the door or window frame. Finally the old-fashioned clocks without cases and with long cords were brought in and sold at fabulous prices.

Matches had not yet been invented, and fire was made by striking a piece of flint and steel, or the back of a jack-knife, together, causing a spark, which was caught in a piece of *punk*, an inflammable substance, formed from decayed wood, which was always kept in supply.

" Borrowing fire," as it was called, was not an unfrequent occurrence.

—Wooden pails were substituted for tin, and wooden plates (called " trenchers "), bowls, etc., for earthenware. Wooden spoons and forks, also pewter plates, spoons and other table pieces were in use.

—Sap troughs were substituted for cradles, and brooms were made out of young hickories.

Farming implements were very imperfect, as compared with those of modern invention. A plow was used with one handle, and a wooden mould board ; a crotched sapling with holes bored through, and supplied with wooden pins, answered as a harrow. Grain was sometimes " brushed in," by dragging a hemlock bush over the ground ; pitch-forks and hoes were manufactured by blacksmiths, and were very clumsy articles ; grain was threshed with flails, and cleaned by shaking it with a " hand-fan," a very laborious task. Fanning mills were not introduced till about 1825.

In lieu of a wagon, long sleds were generally used in hauling hay and grain, and in making trips to mill. Sometimes, however, hay was hauled to the stack by placing a bunch or more upon a brush, which formed a sort of sled ; and not unfrequently carried by two men, for some distance, by running two poles under a bunch, with a man at each end.

Logging and chopping bees were common, and the men and boys most cheerfully turned out with their ox-teams, or came with their axes to assist their neighbor in getting a start " On such an occasion, a sheep would be killed, and boiled mutton and pot-pie had in abundance, for dinner and supper."

Spinning bees were also in fashion. The lady getting up the bee, would distribute tow among her lady friends, and on a day set apart, they would bring in their skeins and enjoy a visit and supper with her. The affair generally wound up in the evening by a dance, or " snap-and-wink-em," and other games. Sometimes, however, the ladies would take their spinning-wheels under their arms and go to the house of their friend, do a day's work and enjoy a visit together at the same time.

Quilting and sewing parties were common, and mothers alike came with their needles to assist their friend in need.

Husking bees, apple cuts and *spelling schools* were more of modern date, and *dancing* was the chief entertainment of the young people. Daniel Lyon was the violinist of those days.

Every mother taught her daughter to spin, weave, make garments, make bread, etc., and the young lady that showed herself the best skilled in those branches of housekeeping was the first to find a suitor. How great the change!

Courting is said to have been " short and sweet," and if a young swain afforded a horse he would take his lady love riding by placing her on his horse behind himself. The greatest economy had to be practiced, and the wife vied with her husband in trying to get along. She not only did the work pertaining to the house, but helped to gather the hay and grain, and not unfrequently assisted in the fallow, or the sugar-bush.

The people took great delight in visiting each other, and would generally go on foot, or with ox-sleds. A meal was always had together, the hostess giving the best the house afforded, which was sometimes one thing and sometimes another. The guest never forgot her knitting work or sewing, and would visit and work at the same time. The kitchen was the parlor, sitting-room, and all. There were no castes then, and the old people say—"those were the happiest days we ever saw." One neighbor envied not another, but, on the contrary, did all in his power to encourage and help along. All dwelt together in " brotherly love," living as true men and women, without the bigotry of a selfish nature.

Liquor was always had in abundance at bees, raisings, etc., and was a very common drink—even church members and preachers imbibing. The best could be had for twenty-five cents a gallon, and when a tippler got boosy, he was not a week in getting over it.

Hay was scarce, and cattle fed largely upon browse—the tender shoots of trees, especially of the maple and basswood. Cows roamed in the woods, and were found by the tinkle of the bells, which they wore about their necks. Pigs were fatted upon hickory nuts, or taken to the beechnut woods.

From the above it is very easy to comprehend the following poem, which was very popular, several years ago :

" How wondrous are the changes, Jim,
  Since fifty years ago,
When girls wore dresses made at home
  And boys wore pants of tow;
When shoes were made of cow-hide,
  And socks of our own wool,
And young folks did a half-day's work
  Before and after school.

The ladies sung and danced so gay,
  Beside the spinning-wheel,
And practiced late and early then,
  On spindle swift and reel;
The boys would ride bare back to mill
  A dozen miles or so,
And didn't fear a sun-burnt brow,
  Some fifty years ago.

The people rode to meeting, Jim!
  On bob-sleds or in sleighs,
And wagons rode as easy too,
  As buggies now-a-days;
And oxen answered well to draw,
  'Though now they'd be too slow,
For people lived not half *so fast,*
  Say fifty years ago.

And well do I remember yet
  The Wilson's patent stove,
Which father bought and paid for with
  .Some cloth our folks had wove;
O! how the neighbors wondered
  When we got the thing to go,
They said 'twould bust and kill us all
  'Bout fifty years ago.

Yes, many things are different, Jim,
  From what we used to see

Some ways are altered for the worse
  And some far better be ;
And what on earth we're coming to
  Does any body know ?
For everything has changed so much
  Since fifty years ago."

THE HUSKING BEE.

" In early times social life, was all aglow, and sometimes
' fun was fast and furious '—the quiltings, raisings, loging-
bees, apple-cuts, and times of neighborhood gathering were
times of great social and convivial talkativeness, song and
merriment. The husking had decidedly my boyish prefer-
ence, because of its surroundings and the usual accompani-
ments of the occasion. It will do to think of yet, it was so
delicious ; it will do to describe, if my pen was a pencil, it
would do to enjoy again, just for the sake of the pie. Here
is the husking bee of olden times!

" The corn was stripped from the stalks and hauled by
loads out upon a clean grass second growth meadow, and
there piled up in a row three or four feet high, six or seven
feet across the base, and from twenty to thirty rods long,
and all prepared for an evening bee. The whole male population of the neighborhood were invited, and usually all
attended if the evening was fine.

" Adjacent to the pile of corn, was a dry pine stub standing
about twenty-five feet high, rich with fat pitchy streaks, and
looked for all the world as if it had stood there on its four-
foot base for fifty years, in anxious expectancy of just this

occasion. At dusk fire about is communicated to the top of the stub and a beautiful light beams forth in full harmony with the evening's pastime. The owner of the pile of corn takes his seat, as soon as he has made husks to sit on, husks his corn, and throws it over the pile in front of him, into clean ground, and all the neighbors come and do as he is doing.

" Soon the pile is strung with busy men from end to end, each man full of talk, the news of the day, deaths, births, marriages, thefts, politics, crops, prices of grain, goods and land; the abundance of game, the success of the recent hunt; and the probability of the next wedding. But hark! hear those ears of corn fall on the pile over in front. A perfect storm, a bushel a minute is a small estimate now, say five bushels and we would be nearer the mark. Hands work, corn flies, and tongues move, time speeds, and the work is being done with a will. Half an hour has passed in this busy way, when the voice of the old gray-haired veteran owner of the pile of corn, rings out upon the still atmosphere of the evening, in a stentorian' sound, ' boys the jug, the jug, pass that jug,' and in a moment the jug is started ; handed along from hand to hand, and from mouth to mouth along the entire pile, until each man has taken a moderate sip of the pure ' Old Rye,' just from the stillhouse, and no corn in it in those days. This was repeated about once in every half hour through the entire evening, and yet they did not get drunk, ' but just had plenty.'

" How beautifully the stub burned, and how fast time flew I cannot now tell, I hear a voice calling for a song, a song, and in a moment a clear masculine voice rings out upon the evening atmosphere far surpassing many of our modern operatic performances, while all listen and all husk. It seems to me as if I could almost hear them now, as they sung, each man his favorite piece, such as ' Barbara Allen,' ' Kate and the Cows Hide,' battle of ' Lake Champlain,' ' Perry's Victory,' ' The Jolly Plow Boy,' and sometimes ' Old Hundred ' would be sung with a zest that showed that devotion was not at all left behind by the puritanic mass. Now finally as a closing song we will hear them sing the battle and victory of New Orleans. Hear it :

> " General Jackson on such occasions lucky ;
> Soon round the General flocked,
> With rifles ready cocked
> The hunters of old Kentucky."

CHORUS.
" Every man was half a horn and half an Alligator."

" This would generally bring down the whole field with shouts and yells in perfect keeping with the old Jacksontonian times ; storm after storm of applause either to the song or the General, it made no difference, the people felt patriotic, and must find vent in some direction. Shout they would and shout they did to their hearts utmost satisfaction. It is now ten o'clock or a trifle later, when it is announced that the corn is all husked, and all the men rise up, repair to the brilliant light around the remaining stump of the stub, and take a good finishing ' imbibe ' from the old stone jug. Here a few wrestling matches are enjoyed, where some of the young experts try their skill to the mirth and merriment of all.

" Just about here the old veteran of crops and field, steps
to the front with his hat in his hand, his iron-gray locks
shining in the light of the stub, and in a moment all is still.
He thanks all present for their presence and help, hopes
soon to have an opportunity to reciprocate the favor, assures
them 'one and all' that he will not be slow to respond to
an invitation of the kind, and concludes his truly native elo-
quence by inviting all men and boys forthwith to his house
for some refreshments ' come on boys, come all.'

" At the house : it was a large double log-house in those
days, and a place of comfort, quietude and repose. The
luxuries of life were dispensed with, while the necessaries
were fully enjoyed. That old fashioned fire-place, large and
ample, with its ample maplewood fire, dispensing both light
and heat ; the cheerful and tidy appearance of all within,
told plainly of days of sturdy integrity, industry and thrift.

" The Matron of the house with her daughters had anticipated the occasion fully, all was in readiness, cheerfulness
and moderate quietude ; that well starched cap on the mother's head, those nice white clean aprons worn by the daughters, as well as the tables loaded with the substantial cook-
ery of the times, all told of the times, the occasion, and of a
good hearty welcome. All are invited to eat, as there are
passed around, doughnuts, apple-pies, pumpkin-pies, berry-
pies, cheese and cider almost new ; and all eat as if they had
not devoured anything before for days. See that boy in
the act of craming a large piece of pumpkin-pie into his
mouth, until he has daubed both his nose and his chin, and
appears to wish that his mouth and throat were both larger.

Oh, those delicious pies, the cakes would almost melt in
your mouth ; why cannot our wives and daughters make
such pies and cakes ? Is it because we have lost our boyish taste and avidity ? I guess that it must be so. The
old men told their best stories ; another song was sung, all
were pleased and all went home feeling fine."

MISCELLANEOUS.

THE PANTHER SONG.*

When back I look on forty years
    With scenes all spread before me,
" 'Tis there I find, brought to my mind,
    Undaunted scenes of glory ;
With settlements new, and settlers few
    E'en settlements were scanty,
With here and there a huge log hut,
    Much like the Irish shanty.

Chorus.—   Who ! peddy-pe-dow,
        Who ! how-de-how, gee up,
        Adap, Aloop.

Those huts of logs, and rude fenced fields,
    Contained our earthly all, sirs
We were content, and onward bent

*The above song refers to the story as told on page 81, which modifies it slightly from the
way it was first given us. The poetry is undoubtedly accurate, and was composed by Eliphalet
Mason. The chorus has reference to the words Mr. French used to repeat when driving his
oxen, and was added by Hiram Cranmer. The song is sung to the tune of "Billy O'Rourke."
French found the young panthers back of Greenwood, on the farm now occupied by Harry
Dorsey. He was living where Greenwood now is at the time. After returning from the East
Mr. French purchased a farm on the hills back of Monroe, and lived there until the time of
his death. Log chains were very scarce, and as stated in the song, he brought one in upon
his back with the traps. He became quite a noted trapper, and as told in the second story on
page 81, after his mishap, instead of returning home, he took across the mountains to Wilkes-
Barre to get his gun repaired. His family became alarmed and the neighbors turned out to
search for him before he returned. Mrs. French is yet living, at an advanced age.

Although our means were small;
The older hands cut down the trees
The younger trimmed the boughs
And when the sun sank in the West
We hunted up the cows.

A chubby boy just in his teens,
The hero of my story,
A daring feat did thus transact
Which ended in his glory;
While at his task a hunting cows
And through the thicket peeping
There he espied on a mossy bed,
Two pretty kits a sleeping.

What do ye there, ye little elves,
I think you worth a grabbing,
So he took them both into his arms
To bear them to his cabin;
Those little kits both scratched and bit
And kept a constant howling
And soon a dismal noise was heard,
The older one was growling.

Without delay, soon found her way
And bounded in before him,
Spit in his face, cat-like disgrace
With a look not much imploring;
And now so vexed and sorely scratched,
One kit he threw its mother
Take that yourself, you growling elf
And I will keep the other.

And now content each party grew,
Our hero home did scamper
The panther grew, our hero, too,
From chubby boy to yeoman,
Witha panther's pack upon his back
He turned a panther showman.

Now many a day, far, far away
  His money grew in measure,
He thought of home no more to roam
  And sold the little treasure ;
Thus sixty more, adds to his store,
  Likewise a hunter's trap,
And a log chain, too, both good and new
  He laid upon his back.

His home he sought, his land he bought.
  And paid for with his treasure
Industrious wages crowned all his days,
  He lived in peace and pleasure :
If you would know, how wealth can grow
  Our hero has an answer
All he has got fell to his lot,—
  By catching the panther.

———

The first assessment of Monroe was made in the winter of 1821-22 by John B. Hinman. The following are extracts : The whole number of taxables residing in the town (then including parts of Towanda and Asylum), 114; the whole amount of tax, on real and personal property, $175.53, the rate of taxation being five mills; the whole number of acres improved, 683, or one thirty-fifth of the township; the greatest number of acres improved by any one tax-payer, A. C. Rockwell, 75. The greatest tax was that of Austin and Russell Fowler, who were assessed upon property as follows:

30 acres improved	$ 350
270 acres unimproved	270
4 houses	400
1 grist mill	400
1 saw mill	200

½ distillery	87
Tavern	75
Fulling mill	400
2 horses	60
2 oxen	50
6 cows	66
	———
Total	$2358

The saw mills in operation in Monroe in 1821 were Fowler Bros.', James Lewis', Eliphalet Mason's and William Means' (on the Vangorder place); the grist mills were—Fowler Bros.' and William Means'; distillery—Fowler Bros. & Bristol's.

From the assessment taken of Towanda township in 1813, (then including Monroe), we extract the following :

Russell Fowler, 1 grist mill, 1 saw mill, ½ distillery; Daniel Gilbert, 1 saw mill; Gurdon Hewitt, 1 saw mill; John D. Sanders, 1 saw mill.

In 1835, the number of mills in operation in the township was 14.

In the *Bradford Gazette* of Sept. 5, 1813, A. V. Mathews advertises for a " laborer on a farm and to occasionally assist in the blacksmith shop."

In the *Gazette* of Sept. 13, 1813, " a reward of $30 is offered for the return of J——— S———, who broke jail on the evening of the 13th inst."

In the *Gazette* of March 5, 1814, John D. Sanders " offers his valuable farm of 440 acres for sale "; and in the issue of Nov. 27, 1815, advertises for " one or two good sawyers."

In the *Gazette* of June 15, 1815, A. C. Rockwell offers a number of grass scythes for sale.

PANTHER STORIES.

" Once upon a time Abner Hinman and Adonijah Alden were coming down the South Branch from Albany, one of them riding a horse, and the other walking, by turns, and when they were passing the Saunders farm (now Ridgeway's) they were somewhat alarmed by the notes of distress which came from one of the herd of cattle that was pasturing in a field that they were passing. The commotion among the cattle, accompanied by the well-known wails of distress, induced the two young men to turn with hurried steps in the direction of the well evinced trouble. They soon discovered a panther with a yearling heifer by the throat, and prostrate bawling for help. The rest of the herd were snorting and blowing, and doing all that they could to frighten the monster away, while he with his prostrate prey, was leisurely drinking the blood as it exuded from the wounded throat. These young men were for once without weapons, but not without the usual frontierman's pluck. They formed the line of attack after this fashion : One on the horse, the other with a stake out of the fence, and " forward all " and " steady on the left," to know who was master of the field. The panther with many growls and grimaces finally quit his meal in great re- luctance, while his helpless victim was released and the cattle driven to a place of safety, and the owners duly informed, and the dogs put on the trail of the imp of the woods. The heifer recovered from the ghastly wound, grew to be a cow, and was afterwards owned by Capt. R. Fowler, for some years being denominated " The old painter-bit cow."

—" Sheffield Wilcox, residing in New Albany, had been

to Monroe to mill, and was returning in those primitive days with his grist on the horse, himself on foot, his coat on his arm and his dog, as a usual accompaniment ; even when they went to meeting he was about. When about a mile south of what is now the Ridgeway farm the dog treed a panther by the road-side, up a tall tree, well out of harm's way—as the panther supposed. But be it remembered that this was that self-same " Uncle Sheff," the Nimrod, the old hunter, then just in his prime, and we have the key to general results.

The grist was deposited at the foot of the tree, his coat laid on the grist, the horse hitched near by, and the dog " Old Carlo," was told to keep a guard, while Uncle Sheff ran three miles to his house in Albany for his rifle, and returned, finding all just about as he had left it. After he had time to breathe a little the panther got the worst of the matter, and was added to the grist as the fruit of a faithful dog, a trusty rifle, and unerring shot."

A BEAR STEALS A FRYING-PAN.

It was in the early part of the present century, when getting out mill stones was quite a lucrative business. Some of the Goffs wishing to share the benefits of this industry, with others went to Mill Stone Run and built a cabin. One evening after they had finished their supper, which among other things included fresh pork, they heard a noise upon the roof of their shanty. Going out to enquire the cause of the sudden move without, they were not a little surprised in seeing a bear with their long-handled frying pan in his mouth, and scampering off to the thicket. They made pursuit, but Bruin was the winner in the race, and carried off the trophy of the contest. He had scented the fresh pork, and thought perhaps that the frying pan contained a choice meal.

THE DISCOVERY OF COAL.

John Wagner and Absalom Carr (others state Edsall Carr) when hunting on Barclay mountain, discovered a black substance in Coal Creek, which they went up some distance, and found coal cropping out. A party went up to see their discovery, among them Jared Leavenworth, who was the first to use the coal for his work. It was first brought down the mountain on sleds, and then reloaded in wagons.

It is said that John Fox hauled the first load to Towanda, and afterward took five tons to Ithaca and sold it for a cutter.

The coal beds at Long Valley were subsequently discovered by John and Nathan Northrup.

The last elk in this part of the country was killed at Long Valley Junction, more than fifty years since by Nathan Northrup.

THE COUNTERFEITERS.

A gang of counterfeiters had a retreat under an overhanging rock up the Millstone run, about a mile above Weston's, where they kept their " spelter "—counterfeit coin. After the organization of the county, the gang was broken up, and the resort abandoned.

We quote the following from Elder Alden's papers, which will show how the people were " duped " with " spelter ": " For a number of years prior to 1814, it was 75 miles to

the seat of justice, and rogues felt comparatively safe, in
what was the western wilds of Pennsylvania ; consequently
Bradford was not peculiarly exempt from those features of
annoyance that are so common in frontier enterprise. A
surveyor's Jacob's-staff was shot off, and his compass down
while he was attempting to locate lands and define their
boundaries. A practicing physician was advised to sell his
horse and invest his proceeds in the " two for one " business, and they would " set him on his feet." " Yes," says
Dr. W., " they did set me on my feet by taking my horse
from between my legs." A smooth tongued sharper ap-
proaches an inhabitant, exhibiting to him a full hand of gen-
uine silver dollars and half dollars, and with great assurance in-
forms the Puritan where such new and shining coins can be
obtained for half price. The unsuspecting man invests five
dollars in the hands of the sharper, and at the stipulated
time receives the ten dollars, all bright with apparent new
coinage, which makes his pockets laugh out almost at the
prosperous increase. Unsuspicious now invests all that he
has, and all that he can find, with all that he can borrow
from his neighbors, and induces those that will not lend to
him, to deposit in this unseen bank for themselves, exhibiting the gains that he has made so easily. In this way the
unsuspecting are induced to contribute largely to this new
money-making institution, and nearly all the available funds
of the whole population are gathered into the hands of the
sharpers in a private way, so that they are now making
their " big haul." If curiosity induces any one to inquire
how this money can be made so easily, or where it can be

obtained, they are given to understand by hints and winks and blinks, that there is a place called the cave or den not far distant and they are easily persuaded, that expert workmen are there at work day and night, making from two to three dollars, all good, out of every dollar there they receive. This shows a dollar gain to the company or workman, and a dollar to the invester, with his original amount returned. It is said to have worked well. The sharpers made a pile in the final strike, and their dupes made empty pockets, and some of them empty homes. Of course, ere the final refunding of the large amount the sharpers were off for Ohio, having divided with their accomplices who were residents, but practically unknown. There could not well be a legal process against the swindlers, for the dupes were ashamed to tell how green they had been, besides having shown downright dishonesty, and in some cases, criminality, in their complicity in the matter. I think that there were never any prosecutions for the ".two for one business," but there were some very eminent scares, that lasted the subjects of them for a life-time. One man fled to Canada, and other operatives in the dishonest matter to the State of New York, while others took refuge in Ohio, and some in the grave. The great scare took place in about 1813, after the organization of the county, and the appointment of all the officers of the law appertaining thereunto. The arrests and prosecutions were chiefly for meddling with counterfeit paper money, which was made in the cities, peddled by agents, and passed by those of questionable honesty. There never was, probably, a set of tools in the county for the successful execution of either hard or paper money. The counterfeiters' cave was used to conceal their spurious coin and bills, as also themselves in times of danger. While the gross amount of their trash was stored in the cave, they were busy in circulating it in smaller quantities throughout the country. Sheriff Rockwell broke up the combination and scattered the counterfeiters to the four winds."

Others state positively that the gang had crucibles and manufactured " spelter." Their tools are said to be somewhere in the town.

AN INTERESTING CHARACTER.

Many of the older people remember " Molly Cole," a wit and demented character that lived at Cole's watering-trough for a time.

She could quote the bible from one cover to the other, almost, and took great pride in attending meetings and correcting the ministers when they misquoted passages. Her habit was to stop the minister, though it might be in the midst of a sermon, and to his great mortification. Her favorite color was white, and she generally wore a white flannel dress, short, with sleeves coming only to her elbows. After ladies' "straw flats," as they were called, had been introduced, wishing to ridicule the new style, she constructed one for herself out of paper, and wore it to church. The words " look at this " had been printed upon the paper, and she took particular pains that the notice stood out conspicuously on the fore part of her bonnet. One day she was met by an acquaintance mounted on a horse, who accosted her rather lugubriously, thus : " Good morning, Molly. How do your sins appear this morning ?" "On horse back, sir," was the quick, incisive reply. She had a garden in which there were two paths, a narrow and a broad one. On both sides of the broad path she had peach trees and at the end she dumped her ashes. The narrow path she said led to Heaven, and the broader one with its temptations (the fruit) to hell. " Mr. ———," she said, " she always found in the broad path ; " implying that he was stealing her fruit, his reward being pictured out before him. Having been mortally offended by 'Squire Gore, she never wore thereafter any "gore" in her dress. She sought revenge and is said to have killed the 'Squire's dog with a wooden sword.

RELIGIOUS.

The Methodists. — It has been almost ninety years since the first Methodist sermon was preached in Monroe, and Elisha Cole was without doubt the first preacher in the township. While yet living in Asylum he came in before his marriage and preached at the house of Henry Salisbury, which became the great centre of Methodism for miles around. It is said that Bishop, Asbury and Lorenzo Dow both preached here, when passing through the county. Among the more prominent of the early Methodist preachers were Loring Grant, Palmer Roberts, Henry B. Bascum, (afterwards Bishop), John Wilson, Samuel Thompson, Marmaduke Pearce, Abram Dawson. James Gilmore, Daniel Wilcox, John McKean, Selah Stocking, Sophronus Stocking, H. G. Warner, Joseph Towner, Father Rogers, Asa Orcutt, George Evans and Dr. George Peck.

As already stated, Rev. Elisha Cole must be recognized as

the father of Methodism in Bradford county. He began his Christian work almost as soon as the first circuit rider appeared in the county, and for two years he appears to have been the only preacher on the Tioga circuit. He had formerly been an itinerant preacher in the States of Maryland and Virginia, but had now settled in Monroe, at what is known as "the watering trough." Here was the nucleus of Methodism in all of this part of the county. There early rallied around this nucleus a band of preachers and laity all of "alike previous faith," who organized an association which has always been known as the Methodist church. Here was the preaching place for years, as also the place for the quarterly meetings. Regular services were held at Mr. Cole's house, he generally preaching himself, but the quarterly meetings in his capacious log barn, on which occasions the Methodists would convene from the Loyal Sock, Athens, Orwell, Wysox, Burlington, Wyalusing, Albany, and from this part of the county, generally. Father Cole's house was superceded by a school house more than fifty years ago. The school house gave place to a tasteful and commodious church edifice, erected at Monroe village in 1839. In addition to the class at Monroeton, a second class was organized at Liberty Corners a half century ago. The first meetings on the hill were held soon after 1816, at the house of Selah Arnout, then for a time at William Wilson's, and once in a while at Abram Fox's. The circuit riders came every four weeks. Among the first were the two Stockings, Bush, Parkhurst, Warner, Wilcox and Evans. After Mr. Summers, Hollon and others came to the hill there were enough to form a class, which was organized in about 1837 by John Wilson, the original members being—Jeremiah Hollon (class leader) and wife, Wm. Wilson and wife, Mrs. Reed Irvine and Francis Bull and wife. Some of the first preachers from 1834, inclusive, were—Joseph Towner, John Wilson, Elisha Bibbins, Benjamin Ellis, Father Mansfield, Rev. Chace and Edward Hodgekiss. Meetings were frequently held at Mr. Summer's and Mr. Hollon's, then in the school house, and finally in the neat and spacious church edifice which was erected and dedicated to God in 1859. The Liberty Corners M. E. church is one of the strongest in the county.

The Presbyterians.—The first to preach Presbyterianism in Monroe, was Rev. M. M. York, of Wysox, who began his visits thereto in about 1809. He, like father Cole, must be placed in the fore-ground of the pioneer preachers of his denomination. "He was a man of fair education for the times, of more than ordinary talent, untiring in his industries, faithful to his convictions, outspoken in his sentiments, and greatly beloved by his people." Services were generally held at private houses and subsequently school houses, before the erection of the church edifice at Monroeton. Before a church was organized at Towanda or Monroe, the professors of this faith not unfrequently attended meetings at Wysox. The Presbyterian church at Monroeton was organized Nov. 25, 1851, and consisted of twenty-five members, all of whom had been members of the Presbyterian church at Towanda. J. B. Hinman, William North and G. E. Arnout were the first Elders. The church enjoyed the ministrations of Rev. L. W. Chapman, for the first four years, and he was

followed by Rev. James McWilliams, after four years he was succeeded by Rev. Darius Williams who also remained four years. In 1862 Rev. Hallock Armstrong assumed charge of the congregation, he being succeeded by the present pastor, Rev. P. S. Kohler. Among the first members may be named, the Fowlers, Mr. and Mrs. Jared Woodruff, Mrs. A. C. Rockwell, Samuel Cranmer, Father Rockwell (the father of Abner C.), Mrs. George Irvine, Mrs. Robert Bull, Selah Arnout Mrs. Geo. Arnout, "Sally Foster," and Amy Sweet.

The Baptists.—This denomination dates back, nearly as far as Presbyterianism in Monroe. Among the first preachers is remembered Levi Baldwin. In 1837, Isaac D. Jones gathered the scattered Baptists on and near the lower end of Towanda Creek, formerly " Franklin and Monroe Church." The Monroe members became a branch in 1838. In 1840 they divided, and Monroe joined the Bradford Association with 37 members. In 1841, the church took the name " Monroe and Towanda." In 1846, Towanda became a separate church. September 18, 1869, the deacons and most of the members having removed from Monroeton, the remaining members voted to disband. Under Elder Spratt's pastorate, they built a parsonage, (1840), now the residence of Henry Myer, which was sold on his removal, and in 1855, they bought the former Universalist meeting house in Monroeton. Upon disbanding they sold the meeting house (now occupied by Mrs. Philo Mingos) and paid the proceeds on the meeting house repairs in Towanda. After some of the revivals, having no meeting house or resident pastor some of the converts united with other denominations. The following preachers served Monroeton and vicinity as pastors and supplies : Isaac D. Jones, George M. Spratt, Jesse B. Saxton, George W. Stone, William H. King, Jacob Kennedy, Joseph R. Morris, William Lyon, Nathan Calender, Increase Child, S. G. Kim, Robert Dunlap, Charles R. Levering and Benjamin Jones.

The Universalists.—This denomination was established in Monroe in 1837, through the influence of Eliphalet Mason. A church edifice was erected in 1841, and Mr. Mason and his son, G. F. Mason, subscribed nearly two-thirds of the building price of the same. The preachers were George Rogers, Ames and Ashton. In 1843, Silas A. Gibson was the preacher, and continued three years. The society became very much weakened because of removals, in consequence the church was sold to the Baptists, and the church went down. The Masons, Kelloggs, Blackmans, etc., were the leading spirits of this denomination.

EDUCATIONAL.

The first school is said to have been taught in the town in 1801, by Polly Fowler in a log school house in the midst of the hickory orchard, below Widow Rockwell's, on the south side of the creek.

In the summer of 1804, Eliphalet Mason taught in " Reed Brockaway's district "—which is now Monroeton, and again in the winter 1806-7, also the winter of 1813-14.

In the summer of 1814, "Sally Rockwell," subsequently Mrs. Jacob Bowman, Jr., kept a school in Abner Rockwell's corn house. Mrs. Bull says : " There were no writing benches, and attention was given principally to the spelling book," This was Mrs. Bull's first term at school, and she remembers that among her playmates were—Roxy and Zilpha Mason, Isabella Cole, Sally Fowler, Jane Edsall, Sevellon Fowler and Miller Edsall. School was then taught for a couple of winters in a log dwelling upon the Decker place, Sally Rockwell also being the teacher here.

Mary Williams, a Connecticut lady, taught the next school, a summer term, in one part of the log house at Fowlertown, occupied by Sebra Phillips and Simeon Bristol.

Samuel Haskell, a drummer in the war of 1812, taught in a little log house on the creek, between Mr. Alden's and Mr. Rockwell's, some two or three years after Miss Williams. He was most proficient with the use of drum sticks, and is said to have been able to use three of them at a time.

Dr. Goodrich taught a couple of terms on Fowler street, before the log school house was built (about 1821) near the foot of Marcy Hill. This structure was subsequently succeeded by a framed building.

Among the first teachers who taught in the old log school house at Monroeton was "James Crooks, whose old shoes many a boy remembers until this day. He made lasting impressions. The old plank school house which succeeded the log one, is yet standing and is occupied as a residence.

The present school building at Monroeton was built by order of the school board of Monroe township in 1837, and the addition made in 1863. S. W. Alden taught the first school in this building. The first school at Liberty Corners was taught by Celinda Sutton in the summer of 1832 or '33. The school was begun in George Arnout's log barn, and finished in this shingle shop, (now on the place of I. Robbins', both of which are yet standing.') Besides the benches the only other furniture, was a cross-legged table for the teacher and pupils to write on. J. W. Irvine who was a pupil here, remembers the the following who were among his playmates : George and Emily Arnout, John, Mary and Eliza Conley, Clark Cummings, Sylvester Benjamin, and John Heeman. The summer following Caroline Cranmer taught in a log house on the " Watson place," then two terms more in the " Sage House," a log building which stood in a field of now Joseph Bull, several rods below the present school building. The original school house at Liberty Corners was erected on the same ground as now occupied for school purposes in 1837, George Fox being the first teacher. The first school at South Branch was taught by Mary Bowman in 1838.

Eugenia Lyon taught one summer in one apartment of Robert Lewis' wagon-shop. The first school house here was built on the site of the present one not far from 1840.

The branches generally taught were reading, writing and spelling. Then next introduced were arithmetic and geography. Goose-quills were used for pens and making and mending them was a part of the teacher's work. Ink was made from the bark of a soft maple tree with a little copperas and sugar added. The sugar was used to give it a gloss. Problems were not unfrequently worked out upon shingles ; and the teacher or pupils ruled the paper used for copy books. In those days school funds were raised by a rate bill, and the teacher not unfrequently required to take a part of his pay in grain, etc. A lady taught some times for six shillings per week.

MILLS.

Prior to the establishment of mills in Monroe, two or three of the neighbors would put together, and go with boats to Wilkes-Barre to get their grain ground. The first grist mill in the township after the " Indian's mill," was the " tub mill," already referred to, built by King Pool, not far from 1797. Then in about 1803 Rogers Fowler's grist mill succeeded on the same site. Then came those of the more modern improvements at Masontown, Monroeton, and Campbell's Mill on the Blackman place at South Branch.

We conjecture that the first saw-mill was that known as " Needham's Mill," which stood on the South Branch, directly back of the Widow Rice's residence. Here the Wilcoxes worked as early as 1802–3 at lumbering, before moving into Albany. Only the ruins of the mill remained when the Kelloggs came in, 1813. It was built not far from the year 1800, aud is undoubtedly the saw-mill referred to on page 6.

Not long after the construction of this mill a second one was erected at Greenwood, and a third at. Fowlertown. Then came the mills at Vangorder's, Masontown, and John D. Sanders' in about 1811–12. Others sprung up in rapid succession till 1835 when there were no less than fourteen mills in operation in the township. The hills and valleys of Monroe were covered with a primeval forest of the choicest pines, and lumbering was made the great industry for nearly fifty years.

ROADS.

The first means of egress and ingress was by following along the creeks. As early as 1795 the road was laid out up the Towanda Creek.

The old Genessee road was the next outlet passing through Overton, thence crossing the mountains to the West Branch. Then came the old turnpike, which was succeeded by the new. As the town populated roads were made for the accommodation of the settlers.

ELECTIONS AND OFFICERS.

*The first election in Monroe was held at the house of Abner C. Rockwell, October 9, 1821. The names of those that voted at said election were—Adonijah Alden, Wm. Gough, Wm. Coolbaugh, 2d, Samuel More, Charles Brown, Jacob Bowman, Russell Fowler, Eliphalet Mason, Thomas Bowdan, John B. Hinman, Daniel Hawley, Ambrose Smith, Reuben Hale, Timothy Alden, Wm. Vandike, Usual Carter, Samuel Cole, Solomon Cole, Rowland Sweet, Timothy M. Dewers, John Lathrop, Gustavus Holden, Wm. Coolbaugh, Jesse Benjamin, Job Irish, John D. Sanders, Amos Cook, Isaac Manville, John Ackley, George Irvine, Ferguson Wilson, Solamon Tallady, James Northrup, Jacob Ringer, Benjamin Bennett, Moses Warford, Josiah M. Cramner, Noadiah Cranmer, Samuel Cranmer, Solin Benjamin, Abner C. Rockwell. David Benjamin, Jonathan Fowler, John E. Kent, Elisha Cole, Austin Fowler, Frederick Fisher, Ira C. Fowler, John Head, Amos Ackley, Samuel Chilson.

---

*Before the organization of the township the qualified electors were required to go " the old red tavern " at Towanda to vote.

The following composed the election board:

Judges—Charles Brown, Russell Fowler, John B. Hinman, William Means, John Vandike; *Inspectors*—A. C. Rockwell, Jesse Woodruff; *Clerks*—Eliphalet Mason, Jacob Bowman, Ethan Baldwin, William Puyron.

At said election, for *Congress* William Cox Ellis had 13 votes, Thomas Murray, Jr., 33 votes; for *Assembly*—Simon Kinney had 45 votes and Samuel W. Morris 5 votes; of the fourteen candidates for *Sheriff*, George Scott had 28 votes, William Keeler 27, Joseph C. Powell 9, George Hyde 8 At the first Presidential election in 1824, 29 votes (all) were cast for Andrew Jackson. The first set of township officers were chosen in 1822 and were—*Constable*—Ira C. Fowler; *Supervisors*—George Irvine, William Coolbaugh; *Town Clerk* —Eliphalet Mason.

Charles Brown and Eliphalet Mason had previously been appointed Justices-of-the-Peace. With the exception of a couple of years or so, when elections were held at the hotel at Monroeton, Rockwell's (as is now) has been the polling place. The last Presidential vote (1884) of Monroe township and borough was—James G. Blaine, 356; Grover Cleveland, 116; John P. St. John, 6. A very different political complexion from 1824.

The present township officers are:

Justices-of-the-Peace—*Charles Hollon, H. S. Hollon; *Commissioners*—A. G. Northrup, Theron Sweet, Lyman Marcy; *Constable*—Clark Cummings; *Assessor*—Delanson Kellogg; assistants—U. M. Pratt, E. S. Andrews; *School*

*Has held the office continually for twenty-five years. The other Justice is a brother.

Directors—E. S. Andrews, Charles Scott, Freeman Sweet, Lyman Irvine, John Northrup, F. L. Vangorder; *Town Clerk*—Eugene Stevens; *Treasurer*—Winfield Scott; *Auditors* —Samuel Lyon, E. W. Neal, B. K. Benedict; *Collector of Taxes*—William A. Kellogg; *Judge of Election*—H. W. Northrup; *Inspectors*—A. J. Petrey, W. D. Ridgeway.

STORES.

Before goods were sold in the township, the people's wants could in part be supplied at Jacob Burman's, Wm. Means' and S. T. Barstow's at Wysox, who in 1815–1816 advertises " new goods, cheaper than ever offered before." We quote the annexed rates from his ad:

Broad cloth from $3 to $6, flannells from 50cts to 1$; calicoes from 30 cents to 60 cents; winter vestings, from six shillings to $2; shirtings from 40 cents to 60 cents."

As previously stated Eliphalet Mason brought the first goods to what is now Monroe village in 1811, and offered them for sale. It appears that he had no trouble in disposing of his goods, but considerable in making collections. Having invested his entire capital, after his stock became reduced and he went out of the business after two years.

POST OFFICES

*The first office was established at *Monroe*, October 29, 1822, A. C. Rockwell, postmaster, and was changed to *Monreton* July 30, 1829. *Linwood* December 3, 1855, Samuel C. Naglee, postmaster, changed to *Powell* April 1, 1872, E. W. Neal, postmaster.

*Before the office was established at Monrooton the citizens were required to go to Towanda for their mail.

Liberty-corners established September 6, 1856, Joseph Bull, postmaster. In about 1851 a meeting was called by the citizens of Eastern Monroe to adopt measures for the establishment of a post office for their accommodation.

Among the names proposed for the contemplated office, were Irvington, Arnoutville, and Liberty-corners. The last name was finally adopted, and has since the establishment of the office been extended to the whole neighborhood.

South Branch, established December 11, 1863, Chester Carter postmaster.

Each of the above offices now has a daily mail. In the first days of post offices the postage was paid by the one <u>receiving</u> the letter or parcel. By Act of Congress, Feb. 1, 1816, the following rates of postage were established:

For * single letters, any distance not exceeding 40 miles, 8 cents, over 40 miles not exceeding 90, 10 cents, over 90 not exceeding 150, 12½ cents, over 150 not exceeding 300, 17 cents over 300 not exceeding 500, 20 cents, over 500, 25 cents.

The same can now be carried to any part of the United States, for two cents. Double and triple letters were double and triple the above rates.

A farther history of the stores will be given in connection with Monroe village. The first to engage in the mercantile business at Liberty Corners were John and Levi Ennis, folowed in 1868 by J. W. Irviné and Jno. Summers. In 1871,

---

*Single letters were those that contained one piece of paper, double letters two pieces, triple letters, three pieces etc.

Mr. Irvine bought out the interest of Mr. Summers and has continued the business alone ever since.

HOTELS.

The first house of entertainment was "Doerty's tavern," then followed successively by Mathews, Fowlers' and Rockwell's.

DISTILLERIES.

As already stated the first distillery was that of Eliphalet Mason, subsequently without doubt, operated by the Fowler's. Rockwell's, Brown's, Blackman's, etc., have already been mentioned.

PHYSICIANS.

As early as 1804 Dr. Lawrence was located at Monroe, then, followed Dr. Mills, Mandeville and Ingham.

CEMETERIES.

Nearly all the heroic pioneers are buried at Cole's, where a burial was established at a very early day. The first marked grave there is that of Hannah Strickland (infant), 1791. These grounds were established for sepulchral purposes long before the cemetery was located at Towanda, and were used by the people for miles around.

Here lies Rudolph Fox, the first permanent settler of Bradford county, Abner C. Rockwell, the first sheriff of the county, and fully a score of the heroic pioneers and compatriots of the Revolutionary war. However each cemetery contains the sacred remains, of its share of those whose names we shall learn to cherish and hold in grateful rememberance. The cemetery in best repair is that at Liberty Corners, where the first grave (infant son of James R. and Sarah Irvine) was made August 8, 1835.

MILITARY HISTORY.

REVOLUTIONARY HEROES.

Perhaps more of those patriotic "Fathers," who fought for our independence and will forever be reverenced down the ages, repose in Monroe's soil, than in any other township in the county. Almost a score of them and soldiers of the war of 1812, have their final resting place in the historic ground, that we have already sketched. The names of several have been mentioned on preceding pages.

THE WAR OF 1812.

In the second war of American independence a draft was ordered and made in Bradford county, in 1814. Eliphalet Mason, Solomon Tallady, James Northrup, John Ellis, Josiah Cranmer, Aaron Carter, Moses Carter, William French, William, Amos and Humphrey Goff, and perhaps Peter Edsall and others were drafted. In October, at the mouth of the Towanda Creek they built a raft and went down the river to Wilkesbarre, thence to Danville, where after a month's absence they were discharged. Amasa Kellogg, Daniel Lyon, Thomas Lewis and many others, who subsequently settled in the town were in this war.

THE CIVIL WAR.

Monroe was among the foremost in furnishing men for our country's sake, in the dark days of disunion; and her men were among the bravest and truest that wore the blue. Upon many battle fields they did the " old flag" honor, and in not a few hard fought battles, covered themselves with glory, always leaving some of their number with the dead or wounded. Deeds of noble daring won for a number names of honor, that we will cherish more and more, as times goes on ; and as we shall look back upon this cruel war—

" We'll thank them again, who out battles have fought,
Nor forget the high services their sufferings have wrought;
    Will commend them to One who in justice is true,
And thank by our creeds the brave boys in blue."

The Fiftieth Regiment P.V. was recruited in the counties of Berks, Schuylkill, Bradford, Lancaster and Luzerne and rendezvoused at Camp Curtain. Two campanies from Bradford were in this regiment, Captain Wm. T. Telford's (G.) and Captain James B. Ingham's (K.) the first recruited at Towanda and the latter at Monroe. The regiment was organized Sept. 25. 1861, by the choice of Benjamin C, Christ, of Schuylkill county, Colonel ; Thomas S. Brenholtz, of Berks county, Lieutenant-Colonel ; Edward Overton, Jr., of Bradford county, Major. The State colors were presented by Gov. Curtin, October 1. The regiment was mustered out of service July 31st 1865. The *Fiftieth* was especially noted for its gallantry in the many battles in which it participated and for its intense sufferings, which were most nobly borne.

The Fiftieth was in the following engagements:
Hilton Head, S. C., November 7, 1861.
Beaufort, S. C., December 6, 1861.
Battle of Choosaw, S. C., January 1, 1862.
Old Pocotaligo, S. C., May 29, 1862.
Second Bull Run, Va., August 28, 29, 30, 1862.
Chantilly, Va., September 1, 1862.

South Mountain, Md., September 14, 1862.

Antietam, Md., September 17, 1862.

Fredericksburg, Va., December 13, 1862. (Not actively engaged, but in line of battle, under fire all day.)

Siege of Vicksburg, Miss , June 12, to July 4, 1863.

Jackson, Miss., July 16, 17, 1863.

Blue Springs, Tenn., October 10, 1863.

Lenoir Station, Tenn., November 14, 1863.

Campbell Station, Tenn., November 16, 1863.

Siege of Knoxville, Tenn., November 11, to December 5, 1863.

Battle of the Wilderness, Va., May 5, 6, 1864.

Ny River, Va., May 9, 1864.

Spottsylvania Court House, Va., May 12, 1864.

From Spottsylvania Court House to the North Anna, and thence to Cold Harbor, the 50th was almost daily under fire.

Cold Harbor, Va., June 2, 3, 5, 7, 8, 9, 1864.

Petersburg, Va., June 17, 18, 1864.

Mine Explosion, Va., July 30, 1864.

Weldon Railroad, Va., August 19, 20, 1864.

Pegram Farm, Va., September 30, 1864.

Near Petersburg, Va., Oct. 27, 1864.

Fort Steadman, Va., March 25, 1865.

Petersburg, Va., April 2, 3, 1865.

Adams, Isaac N., private, enlisted August 14, 1861 ; re-enlisted January 1, '64 ; deserted March 8, 1864,—veteran.

Albro, Samuel, private, enlisted September 13, 1861 ; mustered out Sept. 29, 1864—expiration of term.

*Members of Company K., unless otherwise mentioned.

Annas, Wm., Jr., private; enlisted Sept. 10, 1864; discharged on surgeon's certificate.

Armstrong, Hallock, Chaplain; enlisted Feb. 24, 1865; mustered out with regiment.

Beam, Charles H., private; enlisted Aug. 10, 1861; mustered out Sept. 29, 1864—expiration of term.

Beam, George E., private; enlisted Sept. 3, 1861; mustered out Sept. 29, 1864—expiration of term.

Beam, Joel M., private; enlisted Sept. 17, 1861; discharged on surgeon's certificate.

Bentley, Thomas, private; enlisted March 29, 1864; mustered out with company.

Bowman, George L., sergeant; enlisted Aug. 10, 1861; promoted to sergeant; died.

Chubbuck, Robert H., private; enlisted Aug. 10, 1861; discharged on surgeon's certificate.

Coolbaugh, Monroe A., private; enlisted Aug. 10, 1861; discharged by order of General Court Martial, 1862.

Corby, William A, private; enlisted Sept. 4, 1861; deserted.

Custer, William M., sergeant; enlisted Aug. 10, 1861; discharged on surgeon's certificate.

Cranmer, Harry, corporal; enlisted Aug. 13, 1863; promoted to corporal; discharged by General Order, June 1, 1865.

Dickinson, Herman G., private; enlisted Sept. 3, 1861; mustered out with company—veteran.

Dunfee, Reed W., musician; enlisted Aug. 10, 1861; promoted to principal musician, April 13, 1865 ; mustered out with regiment—veteran.

English, Orlando, private ; enlisted August 10, 1861 ; wounded ; mustered out to date July 30, 1865.

Foster, John C., private Co., G. ; enlisted March 24, 1864 ; wounded ; died August 7, 1864.

Gale, Eli W., private Co. G. ; enlisted March 26, 1864 ; mustered out with Company.

Goff, Orren W., private ; enlisted August 10, 1861 ; discharged on surgeon's certificate.

Haines, Oscar L., private, enlisted August 14, 1861 ; discharged on surgeon's certificate.

Hartman, John, private Co. H. ; enlisted March 26, 1862 ; not on muster-out roll.

Ingham, James B., Captain ; enlisted August 10, 1861 ; killed at Antietam, September 17, 1862.

Ingham, Joseph S., 1st Lieutenant ; enlisted August 10, 1861 ; promoted to 1st Lieutenant Company B., from 2nd Lieutenant, August 1, 1862 ; resigned November 1, 1862.

Kellogg, Charles H., 1st Lieutenant ; enlisted August 10, 1861 ; died September 1, 1862 ; of wounds received at Bull Run, August 29.

*Kellogg, Delanson, corporal ; enlisted August 10, 1862 ; promoted to corporal from private for meritorious conduct at Pocotaligo ; discharged on surgeon's certificate, December 10, 1862.

---

*In August, 1862, he was on board the *West Point,* the night it collided with the *George Peabody,* and was sunk fifteen minutes thereafter, and was among the number saved, being picked up an hour after the accident.

Kellogg, Alva A., private ; enlisted Aug. 31, 1861 ; killed at Chantilly.

Marcy, Hiram, private Co. G. ; enlisted Sept., 1861; died on board of vessel on Mississippi river, Aug. 5, 1863.

Marcy, Vincent, corporal ; enlisted Aug. 10, 1861 ; discharged on surgeon's certificate.

Maybee, Daniel N., private Co. I. ; enlisted Jan. 14, 1862; killed at Chantilly.

Minard, Silas B., private ; enlisted Jan. 14, 1852 ; died.

Mingos, Welles, private, Co. I. ; enlisted April 14. 1864 ; mustered out with company.

Merithew, George N., 2nd Lieutenant ; enlisted Aug. 10, 61 ; promoted from private to sergeant—to 2d Lieutenant, May 18, '65 ; mustered out with company—veteran.

Myer, Berlin F., private ; enlisted Aug. 10, 1861 ; taken prisoner during Lee's invasion of Pennsylvania but escaped on the following day ; connected with the Commissary Department from the middle of September till expiration of term—Sept. 29, 1864.

Myer, Geo. V., Captain ; enlisted Aug. 10, 1861, as private ; made sergeant upon the organization of the company ; promoted to 1st sergeant Jan. 1, 1863 ; to 2d Lieutenant

*He was in command of his company at the time of his capture, and when a prisoner of war en route to Macon, he and nine others made their escape from the cars. The enemy tracked them for seven days with bloodhounds before recapturing them. They kept hid in swamps during the day and traveled by night. They lived upon mulberries, and hoecake which they procured of the negroes. Mr. Myer escaped a second time, when being taken to Charleston, by cutting through the bottom of the car. After six days in the swamps of South Carolina, he was again taken by a scouting party. He was one of the 600 officers held as prisoners at Charleston, and placed under fire of the Union guns during the siege, to save the city. While here he had the yellow fever with 30 of his companions, and was one of the thirteen that lived.

March 1, 1864; to Captain, Oct. 1, 1864; struck in belt at Campbell Station, inflicting abdominal injuries, also wounded at Spottsylvania in left fore arm, and captured same day; confined at Lynchburg, Va., Macon, Ga., and Charleston, S. C.; paroled Dec. 15, 1864; exchanged Apr. 11, 1864, and rejoined regiment; mustered out with company.

Myer, J. Wesley, private; enlisted Aug. 28, 1861; drowned (see note, Kellogg.)

Northrup, Harry C., private; enlisted Sept. 17, 1861; killed at Bull Run Aug. 29.

Owens, Charles R., private; enlisted Aug. 10, 1861; discharged on surgeon's certificate Feb. 27, 1862, and died soon thereafter at Hilton Head, S. C.

Owens, George W., private Co. G.; enlisted Aug 10, 1861; discharged on surgeon's certificate; also corporal Co. C, 141st P. V., enlisting Aug. 19, 1862, from which he was discharged on surgeon's certificate.

Phinney, Andrew B., private; enlisted Aug. 10, 1861; discharged on surgeon's certificate.

Prentice, Joseph T., sergeant; enlisted Aug. 10, 1861; mustered out with Company—veteran.

Ridgeway, Joseph L., private; enlisted Aug. 10, 1861; discharged on surgeon's certificate.

Robinson, Enoch J., private; enlisted Aug. 10, '61; transferred to U. S. Signal Corps

Sanford, John O., private; enlisted Sept. 3, 1861; prisoner from May 12 to Oct. 14, 1864; discharged May 4, 1865, to date Dec. 21, 1864.

Steel, Edwin H. corporal; entered Sept. 3, 1861; promoted to corporal; killed at Spottsylvania C. H., May 12.

Stroud, James, private Co. G.. enlisted March 8, 1864; killed at Spottsylvania.

Taylor, William K. 1st lieutenant; promoted from sergeant to 1st lieutenant Dec. 4, 1864; mustered out with company.

Tallada, William jr., private Co. I., enlisted Dec. 7, 1861; wounded at Antietam, transferred to 5th U. S. cavalry; killed Manassas Gap, Va., on July 2, 1863.

Toolan Thomas, private; enlisted Sept. 7, 1861; killed at Cold Harbor, June 7.

Vargason, Richard. private; enlisted Aug. 14, 1861; deserted, Aug. 3, 1862.

Wanck, George W., private; enlisted Sept. 17, 1861; discharged on surgeon's certificate

West, Lorenzo D., private; enlisted Sept. 2, '61, died at Philadelphia, Pa., Dec. 11, '62.

Wickham, Charles, private; enlisted Sept. 17, '61; wounded; discharged—veteran.

Wilson, Reuben, private; enlisted Aug. 10, '64; discharged on surgeon's certificate, Dec. '64; veteran *

The 141st was known as the Bradford regiment, and was organized Aug. 29, 1862, with the following field officers: Henry J. Madill, Colonel; Guy H. Watkins, Lieutenant Colonel; Israel P. Spalding, Major. The One-Hundred and Forty-First was one of the very best regiments mustered into service during the war, and made a record that " old Brad-

---

* Veterans—those that re-enlisted Jan. 1, 1864.

ford " feels most proud of. Of the seven companies recruited in the county, all entering this regiment from Monroe, were in Capt. Abram J. Swart's company (C). This regiment was mustered out of service May 28, 1865.

The principal engagements in which the 141st participated were :

Fredericksburg, Va., Chancellorsville, Va., Gettysburg, Pa., Auburn, Va., Kelly's Ford, Va., Mine Run, Va., Wilderness, Va., Spottsylvania C. H. Va., North Ann, Va., Tolopotomy, Va., Cold Harbor, Va., Assault on Petersburg, Va., Deep Bottom, Va., Reim's Station, Va., Dabney's Mills, Va., Boydton Plank Road, Va., Hatcher's Run, Va., Final Assault on Petersburg, Farmville, Va., Sailor's Creek, Va., and Burksville, Va.

Adams, Lockwood H., private ; enlisted Aug. 19, 1862 ; disharged on surgeon's certificate, Jan. 1, 1863.

Brown, Charles S., private ; enlisted Aug. 27, 1862 ; killed at Chancellorsville May 3, 1863 ; buried at Military Asylum Cemetery, D. C.

Cogensparger, Josiah, private ; enlisted Aug. 19, 1862 ; killed at Gettysburg July 2, 1863.

Cole, Elisha, private ; enlisted Aug. 19, 1862 ; mustered out with Company.

Coolbaugh, Moses M., corporal ; enlisted Aug. 19, '62 ; discharged on surgeon's certificate Jan. 13, '63.

Corby, James, private ; enlisted Aug. 19, 1862 ; wounded at Chancellorsville, May 3, 1863 ; transferred to Veteran Reserve Corps, Sept., 1863.

Cowell, George E., private ; enlisted Aug. 19, 1862 ;

wounded at Chancellorsville May, 3, 1863; transferred to Veteran Reserve Corps, Jan. 16, 1864.

Cummings, Harvey, private; enlisted Aug. 21, 1862; mustered out with company.

Douglass, Frank W., sergeant; enlisted Aug. 19, 1862; promoted from private. Jan. 25, 1864; wounded at Wilderness, May 6, 1864; transferred to 112th company, 2d battalion V. R. C., Feb. 18, 1865; discharged on surgeon's certificate, July 14, 1865.

Edsall, Aaron, private; enlisted Aug. 15, 1864; mustered out with company.

English, Judson, private; enlisted Feb. 11, 1865; transferred to Co. G, 57th P. V., May 28, '65; mustered out June 29, '65.

Goff, Harry G., 2d Lieutenant; enlisted Aug. 25, '62; discharged Nov. 10, '62.

Goff, Warren W., sergeant; enlisted Aug. 19, '62; promoted to sergeant Aug. 25, '62; wounded at Gettysburg July 2, '63; transferred to V. C. R., Oct., '64.

Harris, Enos H., private; enlisted Aug. 19, '62; discharged on surgeon's certificate, '62.

Harris, Henry C., private; enlisted Aug. 19, '62; mustered out with company.

Hendershot, Nathaniel, private; enlisted Aug. 19, '62; discharged on surgeon's certificate, Dec. 22, '62.

Horton, Bishop, sergeant; enlisted Aug. 19, '62; promoted to corporal, Oct. 25, '64; wounded at Spottsylvania C. H., May 12, '74; mustered out with company.

Johnson, Moses, private; enlisted Aug. 19, '62; wounded at Wilderness, May 10, '64; mustered out with company.

Lafey, Thomas, private; enlisted Aug. 21, '62; discharged by General Order, May 15, '65.

McClen, Sylvelon M., musician; enlisted Aug. 19, '62; captured at Chancellorsville, May 3, '63; confined at Libby prison; returned to regiment, Oct. 27, '63; mustered out with company.

Nichols, Charles E., private; enlisted Aug. 19, '62; died at Falmouth, Va., Feb. 12, '63.

Piatt, James, M., private; enlisted Aug. 19, '62; wounded at Chancellorsville, May 3, '63; discharged by General Order, June 2, '65.

Rice, Joel, private; enlisted Aug. 19, '62; discharged on surgeon's certificate June 1, '63.

Rice, Melvin, private; enlisted Aug. 19, '62; transferred to Co. F, 57th P. V.

Ridgeway, James C., private; enlisted Feb. 1, '65; transferred to Co G, 57th, P. V.; mustered out with company June 29, '65.

Robinson Dana, private; enlisted Aug. 19, '62; mustered out with company.

Schoonover Daniel, sergeant; enlisted Aug., '62; wounded at Chancellorsville May 3, '63; promoted to corporal Aug. 25, '62; to sergeant March 1, '65; mustered out with company.

Scott, Charles, 1st Lieut.; enlisted Aug. 19, '62; wounded in right shoulder at Gettysburg July 2, '63, and in right hip at Petersburg June 18, '64; promoted from private to corporal Nov. 13, '62; to 3d sergeant color bearer Sept '63; to 1st sergeant June 30, '64; commissioned 1st Lieutenant, but not mustered; discharged by reasons of wounds, Jan. 20, '65.

Stage, George, private, enlisted Aug. 19, '62; missing in action at Petersburg, May 25, '65.

Swart, Abram, J., captain; enlisted Aug. 25, '62; killed at Chancellorsville, May 3, '63.

Sweet, Dallas, J., sergeant; enlisted Aug. 19, '62; promoted to corporal June 30, 64, to sergeant March 20, '65; mustered out with company.

Tallada, Jackson, private, enlisted Aug. 19, '62; discharged.

Walker, Elery, C., private, enlisted Aug. 19, '62; wounded at Chancellorsville, May 3, '63; transferred to V. R. C., March 16, 64.

Wanck, Benjamin, F., private; enlisted Aug. 27, wounded at Gettysburg, July 2, '63; discharged on surgeons certificate' Dec. 18, '64.

Wanck, Nicholas, corporal; enlisted Aug. 19, '62; killed at Gettysburg July 2, '62.

The Eightieth Regiment, Seventh cavalry, was raised in the months of August and September '61, two companies B and C., being mainly from Bradford county. A regimental organization was effected at Camp Curtin with the following field officers: George C. Wynkoop, of Pottsville, Colonel; William B. Sipes, of Philadelphia, Lieutenant Colonel; James J. Siebert, of Philadelphia, James Given, of West Chester, and John E. Wynkoop, of Pottsville, Majors. The State colors were presented by Governor Curtin on the 18th of December. During the four years of service, the 7th cavalry participated in 106 engagements and skirmishes. The ten memorable sabre charges, made by it were—*Lebanon*, Tenn., May 5, '62; *Sparta*, Tenn., June 27, '62; *Stone River*, Tenn., Jan. 3, '63; *Unionville*, Tenn., March 4, '63; *Franklin*, Tenn., March 5, '63; *Middletown*, Tenn., May 22, '63; *Shelbyville*, Tenn., June 27, '63; *Noonday Church*, Ga., July '64; *Coosa River*, Ga., Oct. 13, '64; *Rome*, Ga. The regiment was mustered out of service Aug. 13, '65.

The following were members of Co. B.:

Cox, Hiram W., private; enlisted Sept. 21, '61; captured; died at Andersonville, Ga., Aug. 14, '64; grave 5,633.

†*Cox, Rogers*, private; enlisted Sept. 21, '61; wounded at Murfreesboro, Tenn., July 13, '62, and captured same day; . discharged on surgeon's certificate, Sept. '62.

Cox, Usual M., private; enlisted Sept. 21, '61; discharged on surgeon's certificate, June, '62. Also a member of 34th N. Y. Independent Battery, enlisting Mar 29, '62; discharged by General Order, June 26, '65.

Cranmer, George W., private; enlisted Sept. 21, '61; transferred to V. R. C., April, '63.

Cranmer, Edwin, private; enlisted Sept. 21, '61; wounded at Stone River, Jan. 1, '63; transferred to V. R. C., Apr., '63.

Martin, Benjamin, J., private; enlisted Sept. 21, 1861; killed at Jonesboro, Ga., Aug. 12, '64—veteran.

---

†Mr. Cox received no less than 13 buckshot wounds, five shot passing through his left hand, two through his left shoulder, one through his neck, another knocking out two teeth, one through his leg, with three wounds in the breast, and two slight wounds in the left side.

Merick, George, W., private; enlisted Sept. 21, '61; mustered out with company Aug. 23, '65—veteran.

Moe, Augustus, R., sergeant; enlisted Sept. 21, '61; discharged on surgeon's certificate June '62.

Northrop, Chester, ——— captured—

Northrup, Walter, private; enlisted Sept. 21, '61; wounded at Murfreesboro July 12, '62; mustered out with company Aug. 23, '65.

Pratt, Robert L. corporal; enlisted Sept. 21 '61; died at Louisville, Ky., April, '62.

*Summers, John H., brevet captain; enlisted Sept 21, '61: promoted from 1st sergeant to 2nd Lieutenant March 1, '64, to 1st lieutenant Dec. 15, '64; mustered out with company Aug. 23, '65—veteran.

Tallada, Goodrich, private; enlisted Feb. 29, '64; prisoner from Oct. 1, '64 to March 25, '65; discharged May 19, '65.

Tallada, Henry, private; enlisted Sept. 21, 61; died at Euphala, Ga., about June 28, '65.

Tallada, Jackson, private; enlisted Aug. 30, '64; discharged by General Order, June 25, '65.

Tallada, James, private; enlisted Jan. 1, '64; mustered out with company.

---

*Mr. Summers has a most notable and honorable record. Entering Company B as a private, by meritorious conduct he earned the place of brevet captain, before the close of the war, and commanded his company for the last eighteen months of its service. He participated in 102 engagements and skirmishes, had three horses shot from under him, and his saber belt shot off, and yet escaped without a wound, or being captured, during the four years he was fighting for his country. At Lovejoy Station, Ga, he with a company of fifty men ran into the rebel works, and all save he and Orlando Wayman were captured. Even their escape was very narrow, having had their horses shot from under them, and being saved only by taking to their heels.

Tallada, Jewell, private; enlisted Sept. 21, '61; absent, sick at muster out—veteran.

Vanauken, Silas O., private Co. C.; enlisted Feb. 21, '64; mustered out Aug. 23, '65.

MISCELLANEOUS.

Arnout, George E., private, Co. II., 188th N. Y. V.; enlisted Sept., 1864; died Dec. 9, '64.

Arnout, Theodore, private, Co. E., 147th P. V.; enlisted Feb., '64; mustered out with company. July 15, '65.

Allen, Amasa.

Boice, Peter, private, Co. C., 57th P. V.; enlisted Oct. 25, '61; captured; died at Richmond, Va., Feb. 20, '64.

Brown, James.

Baker, Levi C., private, Co. F., 34th, P. V., Fifth Reserves; enlisted June 21, '61; mustered out with company, June 11, '64.

Coolbaugh, Portus private Co. C, 107th P. V.; enlisted March 1, '62; discharged expiration of term, March 2, '65

Chubbuck, Harridon P., private Co. F., 34th P. V., Fifth Reserves; enlisted June 21, '61; mustered out with company June 11. '64.

Chilson, J. Wesley, private Pa. Independent Battery C; enlisted March 30, '64; discharged on surgeon's certificate Feb. 24, '65.

Cranmer, Wallace E., private Co. F, 34th P. V. Fifth Reserves; enlisted June 21, '61; transferred to U. S. Artillery Nov. 24, '62.

Clebern, Jeremiah—colored regiment.

Cranmer, Hiram.

Cranmer, Perry—bayoneted; killed on field.

Edsall, George—Discharged on surgeon's certificate.

English, John M.

English William—10th U. S. I.—wounded.

Ennis, Dayton, Co. E., 5th P. V. R. C.; died Aug. 9, '62, of wounds received in the Seven Days' fight before Richmond.

Ennis, Levi, private Co. K., First Penn'a Rifles; enlisted May 15, '61; wounded at Gettysburg; mustered out with company.

Denton, Isaac, private, Co. F., 34th P. V., 5th Reserves; enlisted June 21, '61; mustered out with company, June 11, '64.

Dubois, Delos, private, Co. I., 35th P. V., 6th Reserves; enlisted Oct. 8, '61; transferred to 191st P. V., May 31, '64 —veteran.

Harris, James, ———, Co. B., 179th N. Y. V.; enlisted March 31, '64; wounded with loss of arm.

Harvey, J. Wesley, private, Co. F., 34th P. V., 5th Reserves; enlisted June 21, '61; mustered out with company, June 11, '64.

Hicks, Jesse, private, Co. I., 35th P. V., 6th Reserves; enlisted July 29, '61; discharged Sept. 26, '61, for accidental wounds.

Huntley, Wallace, private, Co. A., 207th P. V.; enlisted Aug. 29, 1864; wounded at Petersburg, Va., Apr. 2, '65; died.

Hicks, George W., ———, Co. B., 10th U. S.; fell at the battle of the Wilderness, May 6, '64, where he is buried.

Huntley, Daniel.

Huntley, William.

Irvine, Lyman, clerk to Quartermaster.

Jacoby, Peter.

Mason, David.

Maybee, Albert.

Miller, John F., private Co. F. 34th P. V. Fifth Reserves ; enlisted June 21, 1861 ; mustered out with Co. June 11, 1864.

Mullen, Edwin C., private Co F, 34th P. V., Fifth Reserves; enlisted June 21, '61 ; wounded at Spottsylvania C. H, May 10, '64 ; died Sept. 13, '64 ; buried in National Cemetery, Arlington, Va.

Marcy, Solon, private Battery G, First Artillery (43d Regiment, P. V.) ; enlisted March 25, '64 ; mustered out with battery June 29, '65.

· *Monahan, Dennis*—U. S. Battery.

Magill, Edward, private Co. C, 107th P. V.; enlisted March 1, '62 ; discharged on surgeon's certificate Nov. 17, '62.

Merithew, Stanley S., private, 34th N. Y. Independent Battery ;* enlisted March 29, 1862 ; promoted to Lance Corporal ; discharged by General Order June 26, 1865.

Mingos, Edward E., private, Co. H , 188 N. Y. V.; enlisted September 14, 1864 ; wounded in left hand, with its loss, almost, in front of Petersburg, Va., February 6, 1865 ; discharged on surgeon's certificate May 18, 1865.

Morris, Leonard, 1st Sergeant Co. B , 179th N. Y. V.; enlisted March 31, 1864 ; promoted to First Sergeant from

*This battery led in the " Grand Review " at Washington.

Second Sergeant; discharged by General Order June 8, 1865. (For several years engaged in the hotel business, and at present the popular proprietor of the Elwell House, Towanda, Pa.)

McClen, James, U. S. Infantry.

Mansfield, Josiah.

Nichols, Kelsey,—discharged on surgeon's certificate.

Northrup, Orlando, private, Co. I., 35th P. V., 6th Reserves; enlisted July 29, '61; transferred to Co. D., 83d P. V., June 10, 1864.

Northrup, Nelson, private Co. H., 57th P. V.; enlisted Feb. 16, 1864; transferred to P. R. C.; discharged July 21, '65.

Northrup, Thomas, private Co. I., 35th P. V., 6th Reserves; enlisted July 29, '61; transferred to Co. D., 83d P. V., June 10, '64.

Northrup, Sevellon,—89th N. Y. V.; wounded.

Obern, Samuel, P., corporal Co. C., 107, P. V.; enlisted March 8, '62; wounded at Five Forks, Va., March 31, '65; absent at muster out—veteran.

Payne, J. Arthur,

Robinson, John, private, Co. F., 34th P. V., 5th Reserves; enlisted June 21, '61; discharged on surgeon's certificate Aug. 27, '62.

Reed, Daniel,—— killed in the first battle, in which he participated, being literally riddled with balls. He proudly said "that he was going to give his life to his country," when he left his friends in Monroe.

Santee, Mahlon, Company B, 10th U. S. Regulars; died at Fort Hamilton, April 25, 1864.

Ridgeway, Henry, not assigned.

Secore Isaac, —— 28th Mass; wounded with loss of leg.

Schutlz, Fred.

Tracy, Dr. George.

Vargason, George.

Wickham Bradley.

Wilcox, Frank, 185th N. Y. V.

Wilcox, Edward White, Emery.

Soldiers who enlisted from other towns but now residents of Monroe:

Bullock, Darius, private Corporal, 141st P. V.; enlisted August 22, 1862; wounded through left lung at Mine Run, Va, November 27, 1863; discharged on surgeon's certificate April 20, 1864 (Towanda).

Cox, William, Co. B., private 207th P. V., (Hillsgrove, Sullivan County).

Lantz, John J., Corporal Co. E., 52d P. V.; enlisted September 18, 1861; promoted to Corporal; discharged May, 1865. Veteran. (Franklin.)

Lewis, James W., private Co. F., 34th P. V., 5th Reserves; enlisted June 21, 1861; mustered out with Company, June 11, 1864.

Chester Peckham, private Co. B. 179th N. Y. V. (See Albany.

Daniel Peckham, private 108th P. V., also C. 141st P. V.; wounded with loss of left thumb, at Johnson's farm, Va., October 3, 1864. (See Albany.)

Rice, F. S., cannonier No. 4, Battery B., 3rd N. Y., Light Artillery; enlisted July 18, 1864; wounded at Savannah

Creek, Ga., August 18, 1864, through left knee and right thigh; discharged July 28, 1865; also member of Co. I., 47th P. V. M. (Franklin.)

Young, Edward B., private Co. F., 12th Wis. V.; enlisted October 14, 1861; re-enlisted January 3, 1864; discharged by General Order July 16, 1865. Veteran.

MONROETON

Is a flourishing village of about 550 persons, and is situated in a picturesque valley on the left bank of the Towanda creek, four miles from the county seat. The State Line & Sullivan Railroad effects its junction here with the Barclay road, making the place an important point in the shipment of lumber, and as a market for the Barclay coal. The village being a natural centre for a large scope of country, it has a thriving trade in general merchandise and farm produce. Prior to 1873, for a number of years Monroe, stood still, if, indeed was not going back. In that year there were but three stores doing business, while there had been as many as seven doing a good trade during the " Lumbering boom." Since the big fire (1873), the town has been growing apace with the most prosperous villages of the county.

The first impetus to Monroe's growth was the opening of the Turnpike in 1819, which brought the place a considerable traveling custom. In about 1820 mills began to multiply, and Monroe being the center, soon became a leading market for lumber and shingles. In 1835, fourteen mills were in operation in the township, besides a number in Albany and Franklin, the lumber from which were marketed here. Making pine shingles became an important industry, and the settlers brought them in with their teams for miles around, and received goods in exchange. The banks of the creek at Monroeton became literally lined with lumber and shingles, and the town, indeed, at one time really enjoyed a more flattering trade than Towanda. Rafts and arks were made up at Monroeton and at the mouth of the creek, and floated down the Susquehanna in the spring.

The lumbering business was the means of establishing stores, which multiplied in rapid succession. In 1831, Fisher & Wilson began business, in 1832 Hanson & Warford, who were followed by the following prominent merchants: Newton & White, D. C. and O. N. Salisbury, A. L. Cranmer, W. H. H. Brown and J. L. Rockwell, G. B. Smith, S. S. Hinman, Smith & Lyon, H. S. & J. H. Phinney, Geo. and H. C. Tracy, J. B. M. Hinman, and Sylvester W. Alden. The greatest trade was in about 1844. The lumbering business began to wane in about 1855, and ceased to be the great industry after 1859. This took away the life of the town, and there being but little trade, a part of her merchants went out of business. Since the establishment of the toy factory, the tannery, and the improvement of the farming community, the town has overcome its set-back, and is now in a most encouraging condition.

In 1857 the Barclay railroad was put through the township, but the town received no particular benefits, until the opening of the State Line and Sullivan in 1871, as freightage was so high, that goods were brought in on wagons from Waverly and Towanda. Monroe was originally surveyed and plotted for a town in 1828 by G. F. Mason, and was made a borough by May Sessions 1855. The borough comprises an area of about 250 acres, and was originally owned by Timothy Pickering, a member of Washington's Cabinet, and Quarter-master-general in the Revolutionary War. The first industry established at Monroeton was the foundry and machine shops by E. F. Young* in 1840. This institution was known as the "old foundry," and was swept away by the "great flood" of July 19, 1850, but rebuilt in the following year. In 1868, H. W. Rockwell, who had been an apprentice in the old foundry, bought out Mr. Young, and continued business until 1871, when M.A. Rockwell was taken into partnership, and the establishment joined with Means' foundry at Towanda, the new firm being styled Means, Rockwell & Co. In 1876, H.W. Rockwell again became the sole owner, and continued business alone until 1882, when M. A. Cranmer was taken into partnership, the firm having since been known as Rockwell & Cranmer. Since the co-partnership of Rockwell & Cranmer the facilities have been greatly enlarged, and new features added. Attention is given to the building of saw-mills, manufacturing plows, stoves, churn powers, etc, together with general repair work, and the manufacture of shingles, lumber dressing, etc. The institution gives employment to sixteen hands.

---

*Mr. Young had been connected with the foundry at Towanda before establishing himself at Monroeton. He was thoroughly acquainted with every department of his business, and soon built up a paying trade, but, as Mrs. Young expresses it, " in two hours' time his financial standing was changed from good circumstances to poverty." Not only were his foundry and machine shops swept away, but his pattern shop, house, barn, and even the land he occupied. When the flood came it tore out dam after dam, and as the waters gathered into one mighty wave it swept all before it and even cut a new channel for some distance at Monroeton.

The Monroe Manufacturing Co., is a very creditable enterprise, which has been established since April last, (1885). The firm consists of O. M. Brock,* H. N. Mullen and E. F. Fowler. Attention is given to the manufacture of nail kegs, lumber dressing, shingle making, and the manufacture of lath, pickets, etc. The facilities are being increased, and it is believed that an extensive business will be developed. Employment is given to fifteen men.

MONROETON DIRECTORY—1885.

Postmaster—P. E. Alden.

Burgess—E. F. Fowler.

Council—J. H. Summers, O. F. Mingos, Theodore Ackley, Zach. Northrup, Walter Bull, G. G DePuy. D. E. Mingos, Secretary.

Justices of the Peace—N. S. Rhineyault, D. M. Hinman.

School Directors—H. W. Rockwell, John Dunfee, Charles Walker, B. A. Cranmer, J. M. Piatt, H. C. Tracy.

Treasurer—H. C. Tracy.

Constable—John Daugherty.

High Constable—Darius Bullock.

Assessor—P. E. Alden.

Assistant Assessors—J. H. Summers, H. C. Tracy.

Auditors—N. S. Rhinevault, C N. Walker, Robert Saterlee.

Election Board—U. L. McClure, Judge; Wm. K. Munn, O. G. Richart, Inspectors

---

*Mr. Brock, the first member of the Company, is the designer of nearly all of the machinery employed in the establishment. Without any mechanical training, he has worked up to be one of the foremost of inventors, and during his twenty years with Hawes Bros., simplified and designed much of their machinery.

Station Agent, Etc.—G. G. DePuy.
Physicians—O. H. Rockwell, W. C. Hull, C. F. Hopkins.

CHURCHES.

Presbyterian—P. S. Kohler, Pastor.
Methodist Episcopal—E. B. Gearhart, Pastor.

SOCIETIES.*

Evergreen Lodge, No. 163 (Masonic);
Monroeton Lodge, No. 137 (I. O. O. F.);
Monroeton Lodge, No. 2083, (K. OF H.).

ENTERTAINMENTS.

Union Band—Jas, Dunfee, leader.
Lantz' Orchestra—J. J. Lantz, Leader.

HOTELS.

Hinman House—G. L. Bull, Proprietor.
Summers House—Chas. G. Smith, Proprietor.

BUSINESS PLACES.

Sweet & Co.—General Merchants.
Summers & Walker—General Merchants.
E. F. Fowler—Hardware, etc.
O. F. Mingos—Groceries, Provisions, etc.
D. M. Hinman—Dry Goods and Millinery.
Charles Tubach—Furniture and Undertaking.
F. F. Lomax—Drugs and Notions.
D. E. Mingos—Confectionery, Fruits, Nuts, etc.
D. Bullock—Confectionary, etc.
Ingham & Mingos—Meat Market, Canned Goods, etc.

*For the history of, see farther along.

John Dunfee & O. J. Richart—Blacksmithing, Wagon-making, etc.

O. L. Dunfee—Carriage-making and Blacksmithing.

Fred S. Sweet—Livery and Boarding Stables.

B. A. Cranmer—Dealer in Coal, Lime, etc.

E. Roberts—Merchant Tailor.

Geo. Chubbuck, W. S. Hollon—Boot and Shoe-making.

A. D. VanGorder—Boot and Shoe Repairing.

Henry Walburn—Blacksmithing.

Mrs. Emma Mingos—Millinery and Dress-making.

Mrs. B. F. Wanck—Dress-making.

J. J. Lantz, Geo. Curry, G. W. Meeker—Tonsorial Artists.

G. W. Meeker—Watch Repairing.

J. Lloyd Rockwell—Dealer in Flour, Feed, etc.

Monroeton also contains a Graded School, employing two teachers.

The first officers of Monroe borough were—*Burgess,* W. H. H. Brown ; *Council,* H. S. Phinney, E. B. Coolbaugh, Anthony Mullen, D. L. Lyon, John Hanson, Abram Fox (Jabez Huntley is given in the election returns, instead of the last two names.) *Secretary,* L. L. Terwilliger ; *Treasurer,* C. M. Knapp; *Street Commissioners,* A. L. Cranmer, S. S. Hinman ; *School Directors,* A. Mullen, Wm. Douglass, J. L. Rockwell, Geo. Smith, O. P. Lyon, Isaac Maybee ; *Constable,* Jas. McGill (minutes show P. Dunfee); *High Constable,* Wm. Neace ; *Overseers of the Poor,* H. S. Phinney, John Hanson ; *Justices of the Peace,* Jos. Homet, J. B. M. Hinman ; *Assessor,* J. B. McGill ; *Election Board,* C. M. Knapp, Judge ; Levi A. Rice, Patrick Dunfee, Inspectors.

The first borough election was held by order of Court June 16, 1855.

Evergreen Lodge, No. 163, was organized through the influence of Eliphalet Mason. The charter was granted March 1, 1819, the officers therein named being Eliphalet Mason, Worshipful Master; Simon Kinney, Senior Warden; Russell Fowler, Junior Warden, " of a Lodge to be named Evergreen Lodge, No. 162, to be held in the town of To- wanda, or within five miles of the same." The places of its gatherings varied from Myersburg to Monroe, to suit the convenience of its members. The charter was surrendered for a short time during the Morgan troubles, but restored again, since which the work has been regularly and duly performed.

Monroeton Lodge No. 137, was chartered Nov. 17, 1845, and instituted Feb. 12, 1846, by David Blair, D. D. G. M. of Lycoming county. The first officers were D. C. Salisbury, N. G.; E. W. Morgan, V. G.; G. F. Mason, Sec'y.; W. H. Strickland, Treas. At the first meeting the following were admitted to memberhip: Anthony Mullen, Henry S. Salis- bury, Wm Gorsline, Jos. B. Smith, Robert Hunter, Eliphalet Mason, Dr. Samuel Huston, Ira H. Stevens, S. S. Hinman, Peter C. Ward, Elias Mathewson, O. D. Satterlee, O. O. Ship- man, Benjamin Wilcox, George Tracy, Jas. H. Wells, Byron Kingsbury, and Wilson Rogers. Gordon F. Mason was admitted by card at the first meeting, and is supposed to have been the first member of the Order in the county. He was also the first D. D. G. M. The lodge was reinstated March 20, 1874, with the following officers: P. Dunfee, N. G.

M. M. Coolbaugh, V. G.; A. Mullen, Sec.; O. M. Brock, Asst. Sec.; J. M. Griggs, Treas. The Past Grands of this Lodge have been D. C. Salisbury Wm. H Strickland, E. W. Morgan, G. F. Mason, Rogers Fowler, J. B. Smith, S. S. Hinman, J. B. Smith, A. L. Cranmer, E. B. Coolbaugh, D. N. Newton, J. V. Wilcox, A. Mullen, M. M. Coolbaugh, E. F. Young, J. M. Griggs, H. G. Fowler, S. W. Alden, O. P. Lyon, A. V. Trout, Russell Fowler, C. M. Knapp, Patrick Dunfee, R. H. Richards, R. R. Rockwell, Ezra Spalding, A. Sterigere, L. Blackman. This is the oldest lodge in the county, and ranks second to none of them. D. D. G. M. John Dunfee, who is gaining some considerable distinction in the order is a member of this lodge.

Monroeton Lodge, No. 2083, was chartered August 27, 1880. The original members were—E. F. Fowler, D. J. Sweet, J. H. Summers, C. N. Walker, L. L. Lyon, N. W. Ross, George Wanck, N. C. Gardner, Theodore Ackley, Vincent Marcy, A. E. Benjamin, W. S. Capach, E. R. Cox, James R. Devoe, W. J. Devoe, F. A. Eagleston, C. A. Fowler, John M. Harvey, John F. Jones, O. F. Mingos, G. W. Mingos, M. Minto, J. Minard, O. H. Rockwell; James Swartwood, H. P. Barnes, M. M. Coolbaugh, D. L. Huntley, D. Kellogg, Benjamin North, George A. Merithew and E. W. Neal.

*Masontown is really a continuation of Monroeton and comprises a population of about 75 persons. Salisbury Mills are here located.

Greenwood, two miles from Monroeton on the Barclay rail-

*So named from the Masons, sketches of whom have been given.

road is pleasantly situated on a point between the Towanda Creek and the Schrader Branch. The village proper, including the tannery population, is about 400. The place contains three stores, besides the tanning Co's store, a hotel, public school, saw mill, blacksmith shop, etc. Greenwood has boomed the last year, no less than 21 houses having been erected.

Near Greenwood are situated on the Towanda creek, the two largest enterprises in the county—the life and hope of Greenwood and Monroeton.

Hawes' Toy Factory, the one giving employment to the greatest number of men and boys, was established in 1869 by G. B. and J. H. Hawes, of Newark, N. J. In that year they came in and purchased the old Ingham factory and converted it into an establishment for the prosecution of their business. In 1866 the factory was burned and rebuilt the same year with greatly increased facilities, which they have improved from time to time. Attention is given to the manufacture of toys of many designs, and a general wood-working business. In 1880, G. B. Hawes retired from the firm of Hawes Brothers, leaving J. H. Hawes the sole owner of the concern. The business gives employment to 100 men and boys, having more than quadrupled since the establishment of the factory.

The Greenwood Tannery employs from 60 to 75 men. This establishment was originally instituted as the Towanda Tanning Company, and was organized in 1867 with the following members: C. L. Ward, President, Jos. Powell, Treasurer and Secretary, J. F. Means, M. C. Mercur, Thos. E. Proctor, Jacob

Dewitt, Jas. B. Howe, Robert H. Sayre, C. S. Russell, John A. Codding, Chas. F. Welles. Operations were begun in the latter part of the same year, the establishment having a capacity of 25,000 hides per year. In 1881, Proctor & Hill became the owners of the business, and have since their purchase increased the facilities one-third. In 1883, and the present year great additions have been made to their establishment. The capacity of the tannery at the present time is two and one-half million pounds of manufactured leather per year, and a consumption of 8,000 tons of bark. They manufacture a goods known as the " Calcutta Buffalo." J. A. Devoe, the Superintendent of the establishment, has been connected with the business for thirteen years.

NOTES.

In 1884, the Weston Oil Co , was organized for the purpose of sinking a well at Weston, believing that that locality contained coal oil. The directors of the Company were F. F. Lyon, W. H. Dodge, Treas. and Sec'y, W. H. Miner, T. W. McKee, Wm. Snyder. The capital stock of the company was divided in 60 whole shares, and operations begun on the place of Nathan Northrup, Jr., June 2, 1884. The well was put down to the depth of 1805 feet, and oil discovered in Feb. 1885, but not in sufficient quantities to develop the enterprise. Accordingly the " hole " was plugged and the well abandoned April 1, 1885.

Many years ago, when R. G. Mason, a lad of fifteen years, was hunting where the bark fields of J. S. Blackman now are, in stepping over a log he placed his foot upon a panther, which was quite as much surprised as he. Springing to his feet, upsetting the young hunter, the animal gave one of his shrill screams, then bounded off in the wilds, not again to be seen. The animal was tracked, but not overtaken. This self-same young Nimrod once counted 17 deer in a single drove.

When Samuel Cranmer came in he brought apple seeds with him, which he had gathered at a cider-press, and planted them after locating in Monroe and thus grew perhaps, the first orchard in the township.

The grist mill at Masontown was begun in 1827, and finished in the fall of 1828. It was a copartnership arrangement, the members of the firm being Russell and Austin Fowler and Eliphalet Mason.

The grist mill at Monrocton was erected by Parks & Hinman in 1859-60.

ADDENDA.

The Irvines—John Irvine was of Scotch parentage, but was born in Ireland, whence he migrated to America. His wife, and not he died in "Cumberland Co." He died upon the homestead in Northumberland Co.

George Irvine Family—After " James Reed " was born—

Mary, Aug. 22, 1807, who first married Peter Arnout, (deceased) and subsequently Robert Bull, of Asylum, whose companionship she yet enjoys. Mrs. Bull is a most estimable lady, and is greatly beloved by old and young alike. Though nearly eighty years of age, she enjoys good health, and is blessed with an excellent memory. Many of the interesting and spicy things found in this volume are her pleasant recollections.

Samuel, January 18, 1810; married Margaret Irvine, of Warren Co., Pa., where he settled and still resides.

William W., April 5, 1812; married Eliza Hollon; occupies a part of the homestead and is a hale old gentleman, greatly esteemed by his neighbors.

Anna, Feb. 23, 1814; married Jos. Bull and lived at Liberty Corners; died April 9, 1881.

George, Nov. 11, 1816; married first Jane Sweet, subsequently Eunice Heverly and occupies a part of the homestead.

Rebecca J., June 28, 1819; never married, resides at Liberty Corners.